BRACED FOR MURDER

This Large Print Book carries the
Seal of Approval of N.A.V.H.

A BEANIE AND CRUISER MYSTERY

Braced for Murder

Introducing Calamity, Cruiser's Canine Partner in Crime

Sue Owens Wright

WHEELER PUBLISHING
A part of Gale, Cengage Learning

Detroit • New York • San Francisco • New Haven, Conn • Waterville, Maine • London

This novel is a work of fiction. Names, characters, places and incidents are either the product of the author's imagination, or, if real, used fictitiously.

Wheeler Publishing Large Print Cozy Mystery.
The text of this Large Print edition is unabridged.
Other aspects of the book may vary from the original edition.
Set in 16 pt. Plantin.

LIBRARY OF CONGRESS CATALOGING-IN-PUBLICATION DATA

Wright, Sue Owens.
Braced for murder : a Beanie and Cruiser mystery, introducing Calamity, Cruiser's canine partner in crime / by Sue Owens Wright. — Large print edition.
pages ; cm. — (Wheeler Publishing large print cozy mystery)
ISBN-13: 978-1-4104-6115-5 (softcover)
ISBN-10: 1-4104-6115-7 (softcover)
1. Women private investigators—Fiction. 2. Dogs—Fiction. 3. Murder—Investigation—Fiction. 4. South Lake Tahoe (Calif.)—Fiction. 5. Large type books. I. Title.
PS3623.R565B73 2013b
813'.6—dc23 2013031941

Published in 2013 by arrangement with Sue Owens Wright

Printed in the United States of America
1 2 3 4 5 17 16 15 14 13

This book is dedicated to all the found hounds and the people who open their hearts and homes to them.

Chapter 1

Writing an exposé on a dog pound can be beastly work, especially for someone like me with an animal attraction. That was the case with a story I was covering for the *Tahoe Tattler* about Lakeside Animal Shelter. Since accepting this freelance assignment, I found myself involved not only in a conflict about the overcrowded, mismanaged facility but also rescuing homeless basset hounds for Found Hounds, a local organization that's dedicated to saving as many bassets as they can from shelters. No one was braced for the pack of trouble about to be unleashed on South Lake Tahoe, at least not until I discovered the corpse.

I'd already helped place several dogs in their forever homes and had volunteered to help out on July 14 at the upcoming Bassetille Day Basset Waddle, a fundraiser for a new no-kill shelter in South Lake Tahoe. My own found hound, Cruiser, who until recently had enjoyed being an only dog, was learning to tolerate living in a hound dog hostel, otherwise known as my mountain cabin in the Tahoe National Forest.

While waiting for a call from a fellow rescuer, Jenna Fairbanks, about another homeless basset that had turned up at the shelter, I busied myself with putting the finishing touches on a raffle prize basket to raise money at the Waddle for Found Hounds. Cruiser was naturally curious about my activity. As always, the slightest crinkle of paper or aluminum foil alerted him to the possibility of treats. A moment later, he was nosing into the contents of my basket for something, anything, tasty to eat.

"Sorry, Cruiser. These goodies aren't for you, boy." I nudged his muzzle aside before he could douse my cleverly arranged basket in drool. You might say that expert basketry runs in my family. Intricately woven baskets from the Washoe tribe are highly prized among collectors of Indian artifacts. Though my gift basket was not one I'd woven myself, I hoped that it would raise some generous bids in the silent auction, assuming a certain treat-nabbing hound didn't claim the prize first.

Cruiser took the hint but didn't stray too far to keep an eye out for anything that might drop within range. I tried my best to ignore "the look" I was getting from The Lord of the Glance. We both knew if he kept up the doe-eyed, pitiful pup act long enough I'd crumble like a soggy dog biscuit and offer him something from my stash of goodies. I have to go easy on the treats with Cruiser or he'll become a round found hound. There's nothing he likes better than to eat. Fortunately, the phone's ringing interrupted the test of wills between Cruiser and his faltering food slave.

"Hi, Elsie. It's Jenna." Her voice sounded hollow on her cell phone, like she was talking into a soup can in a seventh-grade science experiment. "I have more information for you about the dog at Lakeside. Got a pen and paper?"

"Go ahead."

"This one's a tricolor female, about a year old. Her name is Calamity."

"Cute name."

"She was wearing a name tag when she was picked up, but there was no other I.D. on it."

"Probably another tourist lost his dog." Cruiser was one of the few lucky abandoned summer strays that had found a permanent home.

"No doubt," Jenna said. "People come up

here to visit the lake and forget how important it is to put a current address and phone number on their dog's collar."

"Too bad. A little thing like a microchip can save owners and their dogs a lot of distress."

"Especially the dogs!"

"No microchip on Calamity?" I was glad I'd had Doc Heaton implant one in Cruiser during his last visit to the clinic. He could still be the happy wanderer if I didn't watch him closely, and I didn't want him ending up a jailbird. Given half a chance, he'd follow that keen nose of his to the ends of the earth.

"I'm sorry to say they don't routinely check for them at the shelter, but you can have the vet check for one. No one has come to claim her in three days, and no one adopted her over the weekend. Time's up for this dog, unless you can take her until she can be placed in a permanent home."

"I'll take her!"

Cruiser cocked his head and gave me a quizzical look. If there were a cartoon thought bubble over his head, it would have read, *Uh-oh. Better start stashing my treats for a rainy day. Mom's takin' in another refugee.*

"Oh, good. She's in a pen at the rear of

the facility. They'll hold her until ten A.M. If she's not adopted by then . . ."

"I get the picture, Jen."

"When you get to the shelter, look for A . . . body."

"What? Look for a what? You're breaking up. Jenna, you still there?"

"Hold on. . . . driving through Cave Rock."

"Speak up. I can barely hear you." It wasn't the first time this Native American sleuth had encountered trouble because of Cave Rock. My first involvement in Tahoe crime-busting had been over this rock of ages, which is still a sacred site to the Washoe tribe.

All I heard was dead air for a few moments, and then Jenna's voice came through again. "Can you hear me *now?*"

"You sound like a TV cell phone ad. What did you say before?"

"I said look for Amanda Peabody. She's on the staff, but she's sympathetic to our rescue efforts and will help you with Calamity."

"I thought Rhoda Marx usually handles all the adoptions at the shelter."

"She does, but as you know, she's been making it difficult for the rescue groups to do their job."

"Too bad." Rhoda Marx had become a pet adoption roadblock ever since taking over as manager of the shelter. The handling, or mishandling, of stray pets by Round 'em Up Rhoda, as she was known by animal lovers in the community, angered more than local rescue groups.

"Fortunately for Calamity, Rhoda didn't turn up at work today," Jenna said. "Didn't call in sick. A no-show."

"That doesn't sound like the *über* efficient Rhoda I know."

"The stalag probably won't miss having that mutt matron goose-stepping around there for one day."

Even Rhoda's co-workers had occasionally called her Mengele Marx and made other derogatory cracks about the shelter being an animal Auschwitz. She was commonly referred to as a "euthanasia expert." From the numbers of animals destroyed there each year, it appeared she was proud of her reputation. Those comments were well deserved. The fact that she resembled a dreary character from an Edward Gorey cartoon didn't help matters much. Although many of the problems at the shelter were also due to a faltering national economy and efforts to stretching the dollar until the eagle screams for mercy, by Rhoda's failure to implement at least some positive changes at the shelter within a limited budget, she had rightfully earned her reputation.

What had sparked the recent media focus on the shelter was a case in which a basset had been rescued once from the shelter and placed in a loving home, only to end up back at the same facility and destroyed before the rightful owner could claim her pet. Tahoe pet lovers and animal rights groups were outraged over the incident, and it had become the canine cause *du jour.* Letters of protest besieged the *Tattler* when the article ran with the ill-fated hound's sad face on the front page. My editor, Carla Meeks, has never been one to downplay such ready-made drama. Community chaos makes sensational headlines, and that sells newspapers.

In light of the uproar, I wasn't too surprised to hear Rhoda had taken a sick day, unannounced or not. She'd become a public scapegoat over the shelter problems, thanks in no small part to the spotlight trained on them in the paper and on TV, not to mention the efforts of the Tahoe Animal Impoundment Liberation Society (TAILS), a militant group that had staged several protests outside the shelter since the story broke.

A band of activists with roots in the Bay Area, TAILS members were not above proving their point through acts of violence if need be. There had been some incidents at research labs in Northern California, where primates had been freed from their cages to run amok in the community. All were quickly captured, but it could have been disastrous because some of the monkeys were infected with highly contagious diseases.

Cruiser sidled up to me and planted his drool-doused chin on my knee. As any writer and her hound dog knows, perseverance eventually pays off, except in this instance. He wasn't getting any of these Bacon Beggin' Strips. They were reserved for the raffle winner's dog.

The furrows in his brow made him look more pitiful than usual. How can a basset hound look any other way? No botox for bassets. I sensed that this forlorn expression wasn't about treats, though. He knew something was up. It was as if he had understood every word of my conversation with Jenna about the stray basset.

More likely, he was reading my body language and knew I was excited about something, but Cruiser knew all about strays. He'd been one himself before my husband found him abandoned by the side of the road one summer. At first I thought it was a stroke of luck for Cruiser when Tom brought him home, but now I know it's really the other way around. I never saw anyone bond with a dog the way my husband had with Cruiser. They were inseparable, and Cruiser was never happier than when they were doing guy stuff together out in our garage. So was his idol, Tom. Cruiser kept vigil on the world, greeting an occasional passerby or barking at a sassy squirrel while Tom tinkered on projects and the radio played his favorite '60s hits.

I didn't grow up around dogs and neither had my daughter, Nona. Truthfully, I wasn't too receptive at first to the idea of our adopting a stray dog. I'm so glad I didn't say no. My long-eared friend and I have been through a lot together and have provided each other with much-needed solace since Tom died so tragically in a forest fire. I'd have been too lonesome without Cruiser's company, especially since Nona's visits have grown infrequent, with her blossoming career as a fashion model. This cabin of mine can be a bit solitary sometimes, even with a howling basset around.

I didn't know if my slobbery sidekick would adjust to another four-legged guest at the MacBean lodge. Cruiser's an easy-going guy, as his name implies, but he'd made it clear enough in the past that he prefers being an only dog, especially after I brought a golden retriever named Buddy home. Then there was the mischievous Scottish terrier and a pampered Pekingese that took up residence with us briefly during the Sirius murder case, which really messed with his leader-of-the-pack status.

He'd been pretty tolerant of my basset rescue activities thus far, as long as I didn't become a foster flunky and make this a multi-dog household for good. I decided to take Cruiser along with me to the shelter, so he and my new charge could get acquainted away from his home turf and avoid any potential dominance issues that might arise.

I grabbed Cruiser's leash and he followed me to my Jeep, known around here as the BUV, or Basset Utility Vehicle. I boosted his heavy canine caboose onto the passenger seat and belted him into his safety harness. Lifting seventy pounds of hound gets harder as I get older. I may have to get one of those dog ramps so he can waddle right up into the car. Cruiser settled into cruising stance and we were off, headed straight for Calamity at Lakeside Animal Shelter.

CHAPTER 2

A cool alpine zephyr zipped through the car windows. Despite the season, the weather was nippier than a border collie among a herd of unruly sheep. At the topmost elevations, linen clouds draped towering tables of granite. It was the kind of Tahoe summer day I so love, cool and pleasant with a sapphire sky to rival the lake, a royal blue crown jewel of the Sierra. Still, there were clouds gathering on the horizon that signaled a storm in the making, but I'm not just talking about the weather.

As we approached Lakeside Animal Shelter, a cacophony of yips, barks, and howls could be heard a good distance away. I've never liked going to the shelter. It's hard not to come away in tears. Cruiser bayed his answer to the lament coming from within the cold cinderblock walls of the shelter. Several placard-carrying protesters from TAILS circled in the parking lot.

Painted in bloodred letters on the signs were slogans like LAKESIDE KILLING KENNEL and LAKESIDE, THE ANIMALS' ABU GRAIB.

They spotted me driving up with a dog in the car, and I sensed I was about to be confronted. One protester broke from the group and approached me as I got out of the car.

"You're not surrendering your dog to this place, are you?" Her voice was husky, and so was she. She appeared to be in her early twenties and wore combat boots dyed to match the color of her spiky, purple hair. I counted thirteen piercings, and those were just in her left ear.

"Heavens, no!"

Her icy blue gaze conveyed that she didn't believe me. I had to admit it's all too common at pounds and shelters to see people dropping off an old dog with costly health issues or the grown puppy Santa left last Christmas, or the dog whose owners didn't have time for him anymore or couldn't take him along with them to wherever they were moving. I knew the usual assortment of shelter stories; so does every animal shelter worker in America. Everyone wants a puppy, but cute little puppies grow up into dogs that need food, care and attention, and usually don't get spayed or neutered. As dogs age and associated health problems arise, their upkeep gets more expensive. Old Dog Tray ends up dumped at the pound or shelter and usually doesn't get re-homed.

"Trust me, ma'am, you don't want to leave your dog here. It's anything but a shelter. This isn't a fit place for any animal." I knew she was right about that, which was why I was here.

"Trust me, Miss, I'm not planning to drop off my dog."

"The name is Victoria Thatcher. People call me Tori. I'm with TAILS, which stands for . . ."

"I know all about your group. I'm Elsie MacBean. I'm working with Found Hounds to place basset hounds in foster care until they can be adopted."

Her demeanor softened. "Elsie MacBean. Of course! I know who you are. You're a reporter with the *Tattler,* aren't you?"

I nodded. Gee, I didn't even have to flash my press card anymore. People knew me, mostly because of my dog and our past escapades into crime-solving at the lake. Maybe Cruiser and I would have to start wearing disguises in public.

"And this fine fellow here must be the famous Cruiser." She reached in the window and stroked Cruiser's head. He leaned closer so she could scratch his ear. What a pushover.

"That he is. So you see, I'm really here to make a withdrawal, not a deposit."

She laughed. Kewpie Doll dimples creased her cheeks when she smiled, which wasn't often. Tori was sure no Kewpie.

"Great. I wish we could get more people coming in here to adopt dogs and cats from this place."

"Best not scare them away then. Some people are a little nervous about crossing picket lines, you know?"

I'd struck a chord. Hackles rose, and her militant tone resumed.

"We're here to raise public awareness about the problems at this facility and ensure necessary changes are made to improve conditions for the animals."

"Me too, but I prefer to do it in writing."

"Different strokes."

"Precisely."

She was right, of course. Still, I worried that her mutt militia might have the opposite effect intended by discouraging potential adopters. There had already been some graffiti and other vandalism at the shelter that had been attributed to TAILS.

Tori made no excuses or apologies for any

troubles at the shelter. In fact, for the sake of free publicity, she was happy to claim responsibility for them, whether or not her group was the cause. Anything to aim the spotlight of public scrutiny on the shelter, more specifically on Rhoda Marx, was fine and dandy. I suspected she'd only been nice to me in the hope of getting some coverage in the *Tattler*. I would have been happy to do an impromptu interview, but right now a dog needed rescuing.

I left Cruiser in the Jeep in case someone else might assume I was here to surrender him to the shelter. Entering the kennels to search for my latest rescue hound, I could see and smell plenty of cause for complaint. The cages were overcrowded and filthy. There was no food or fresh water in the dispensers. The kennels had not been cleaned recently, and the shelter had already opened to the public for the day. I could only assume that these cages were not intended for public viewing. If they were, it was doubtful anyone would adopt any of the animals impounded in them. In one cage I counted half a dozen dogs of all ages and breeds. There was the usual assortment of discarded pits and Chihuahuas. Puppies ambled playfully between the legs of a Rottweiler, which snarled and snapped an occasional warning.

As I passed another cage, a kennel-crazed Husky paced in circles while an Aussie shepherd gnawed in futility at the chain link fence. One dog had a torn, bloody ear from a fight that had probably erupted with a cellmate. The smell coming from the cages was so bad I held a handkerchief to my nose. For a moment I thought I might be sick.

"Need some help?" I heard a man's voice behind me. I turned to face a kennel attendant with Conan the Barbarian biceps. Did guys pump iron in dog prison, too? A cigarette dangled on his lip under a shrub of mustache. The label affixed to his shirt pocket said REX. Good name for a dog-catcher, I thought, trying not to laugh. At least *he* had an ID tag.

"I'm looking for Amanda Peabody. She's a volunteer here."

"I haven't seen her yet this morning. We opened a few minutes ago."

"Looks as though these cages could use a good cleaning before the public arrives. The smell is kind of off-putting for potential adopters."

"You with that bunch of animal-rights kooks outside?"

"No." I thought it best not to mention I

was doing an exposé in the *Tattler* about the shelter, or he'd have kicked me to the curb with the rest of the animal-rights kooks.

"Good. We've got enough to handle around here without a bunch of troublemakers making things harder for us. What can I do for ya?"

"I'm looking for a dog."

"You've come to the right place, lady. We got plenty of those."

"Too many, from the looks of it."

"We only have so much space for all these strays and not enough funds to keep 'em here for long. You lose a dog?"

"No, someone called and told me you have a basset hound. Female, about a year old."

"Basset hound? Oh, yeah. I remember that one."

"Where is she?"

"In a holding pen . . . at the end of the gray mile." This guy was as bad as Skip with his gallows humor. "This way."

I followed Rex through row upon row of cages, trying not to notice the sea of searching, hopeful eyes that followed me. Every cage held packs of dogs in all sizes and breeds, longhaired, shorthaired, purebreds and mutts, all wanting liberation and love. If I were *bow*lingual, their desperate barking would have translated to "Get us out of here!" I wanted to take them all, but of course I couldn't. I didn't have enough space to start my own kennel. Besides, Cruiser wouldn't hear of it.

Finally, we came to the last row of cages, and like every animal in the shelter, I instinctively understood what awaited them beyond that last wall. A palpable pall of fear and death intermingled with the foul air. I would not be bringing Cruiser inside to meet Calamity. They would have to be introduced elsewhere. I knew it would be far too traumatic for him to enter this place.

"Here she is," Rex said, pointing to a smallish tricolored basset cowering in a far corner of the cage. She had the longest ears I'd ever seen and couldn't have weighed more than thirty pounds. I could count every single rib beneath her dull, dirty coat. If I'd had thimbles I could have played them like a washboard. I tried coaxing her to me with a treat I had stashed in my pocket.

"Calamity. Come, Calamity." She started to respond to me and made a move to approach me until she spotted Rex. Her lips curled in a warning snarl. Clearly, she was afraid of men. I surmised she had been abused by one at some time or other. Not Rex, I hoped. One often never knows the history of a stray, and with some of the stories I'd heard from members of rescue groups, sometimes it's better not to know. "Can you let me inside the cage with her?"

"I'm not really supposed to, but okay," Rex said. "Be careful, though. She's as snappish as a crocodile."

He unlocked the cage and I stepped inside. Calamity still cowered in the corner, refusing to come to me. Her eyes were fixed on Rex, not on me. I wasn't getting a warm and fuzzy vibe from him, either.

"Would you mind leaving us alone for a while? She seems wary of you."

"Yeah, sure. I've got plenty of other work to do."

I didn't ask what kind of work. I only hoped it was cleaning kennels and feeding and watering the hungry inmates at Lakeside Shelter.

I knelt down so I wouldn't appear so overwhelming to the short-legged dog. Ever viewed the world from the knees up? It must be scary. Coming down to her level instantly seemed to ease her apprehension. After a lot of coaxing, Calamity finally came closer to me. She peered into my eyes with hers, which were the rich color of Hershey's dark chocolate. She edged closer. I held the tidbit far enough out so she could get a good whiff. She sniffed it, snatched the treat, along with nearly a finger or two, and retreated to her corner to devour it.

Under the circumstances, it was hard to tell whether she was exhibiting fear aggression because of being caged or if she would display the same behavior on the other side of the fence. She might require a lot of training and socialization before she could be placed with a family, but that's why I was here — to give her a second chance.

I went to fetch Rex and then had him get a leash so I could spring Calamity from pup prison.

"Here, let me have it." He handed the leash to me. I managed to lasso her before she could slip past me.

"They'll handle everything for you up at the front desk. Then she's all yours. Good luck!" Rex seemed glad to be rid of this thirty pounds of tri-trouble.

Despite her small size, she was as strong as an ox. The little, long-eared locomotive dragged me the length of the shelter toward the double doors leading to the exit. Hunkering as close to the ground as she could get, and with a white stripe down her back, she looked more badger than basset. She instinctively knew the way out of the place and wasted no time in getting us there as quickly as possible.

"Be right back!" I managed to yip to the woman at the front counter before Calamity yanked me out the front door, through the picket line, and across the parking lot. She wanted to get as far away from that death camp as she could. I managed to steer her toward the Jeep, and before she could outmaneuver me, I thrust her into yet another wire cage.

Quickly shutting the door of the sky portable kennel before she could realize where she was and try to escape, I slipped her another tasty treat and tried to reassure her everything would be fine now. She seemed to understand I meant her no harm, although she wasn't too happy about being inside a cage again. I'm sure she was glad to be anywhere else but in the shelter. So was I!

Cruiser was curious about what was going on in the back of the Jeep, but my good dog stayed put. This wasn't the first canine hitchhiker we'd had in the car, so he knew the drill.

"You're okay, Calamity. I'll be back in a few minutes." I gave her another couple of treats to distract her, tossed one to Cruiser too, then went back to the checkout counter to complete the paperwork.

While waiting at the counter, I noticed a very large white German shepherd dog curled in a battered basket beside a desk. Then I noticed the name on a brass nameplate on the desktop, Rhoda Marx. He looked up at me when I approached the desk, then sighed and tucked nose to tail again.

"Sorry to keep you waiting," said Amanda Peabody, who had finally materialized after Rex told her I was looking for her. "Busy day."

"Looks like you have your hands full around here."

Amanda looked flustered as she leafed through files searching for the right form. I attributed her anxiety to the demonstrators outside, and her boss's unexpected absence.

"Yes, we're short-staffed, and people are dropping off way too many animals. It's hard to keep up with everything else there is to do here every day."

"That always seems to happen in the summer at Tahoe."

"The usual problems of kitten season and tourists losing or dumping their dogs don't help matters."

"Beautiful dog," I said. "Whose is he?"

Amanda glanced in the direction of the sleeping shepherd. "Oh, that's Spirit. He belongs to Miss Marx. He's sort of the mascot around here. Good watchdog, too. I feel safe with him around, especially with all the troubles lately."

"I imagine so. He must weigh a hundred twenty pounds at least."

"More like a hundred fifty."

"Puts away a lot of dog chow, I'll bet."

"Yes, but he hasn't touched a drop yet today. It's not like him."

"Thank goodness my rescue dog isn't *that* large."

"I'm glad Jenna sent you, Elsie. It didn't look like this little basset was a good candidate for placement, especially after she failed most of her socialization tests. But I understand you have some experience with rescue dogs, so you might be able to rehabilitate her."

"What kind of tests did they give her?" Amanda didn't know that I was interviewing her too, testing her to see if they really did thoroughly test the dogs for their people skills before giving them a thumbs-up or -down for possible adoption. It was hard for me to stop being a reporter, even for a minute.

"We evaluate how they react to being approached, petted, held down on their back. Do they struggle and squirm or submit when you hold them down? It's a good test for puppies, too. If they struggle, you have a dominant dog that might be difficult to train or control. Also, you want to see if they will respond to any of the basic commands — sit, stay, down. Of course, any demonstration of aggression is considered an automatic elimination. We can determine that pretty quickly by squeezing the tender part of the paw. If the dog tries to nip or bite, that's it. They're pretty strict about that rule here."

It seemed a bit unfair to make life-or-death decisions this way. Dogs might perform better on such tests away from these stressful surroundings.

"So, how'd she do?"

"She didn't react very positively to any of our tests."

"I already noticed that she has some behavior issues. How on earth did you get her exempted for fostering?"

"Again, just lucky. The shelter manager has final approval on all adoptions. If she'd seen how this dog reacted to the tests, it would have been curtains for her. Rhoda didn't show up today, though, so I slipped this one through without her knowing about it. She's such a pretty little girl, and I think she could be a good dog in the right home.

Don't blow my cover, okay? I'd lose my job for sure."

"Don't worry, I won't."

"Good, I have a few papers for you to sign, then Calamity is yours." I don't think I imagined the tone of relief I heard in Amanda's voice.

I had finished signing the last of the release papers when my ears were assaulted by a woman's scream that echoed from the far end of the kennel. It could be heard above the frenzied barking and howling of every inmate at Lakeside Animal Shelter.

Amanda and I dashed through the corridors to the source of the hysterical screams. The dogs barked and lunged at the cage doors as we ran past them. Several fights broke out. Even as we reached the far end of the facility, I was still unsure where the sound had come from. Rex abandoned hosing down kennels and the canine combatants inside them and joined us in our search, but the screaming had stopped by the time we arrived. We stood there, listening for another clue of where to look for the source. Someone moaned.

"Did you hear that?" I said.

"Yeah," Amanda said.

Rex pointed to the euthanasia room. "It came from in there."

I'd never before been through the door marked "Kennel Personnel Only," but I knew what went on behind it. Inside the small room was the CO chamber, where the unwanted and the unclaimed met their fate daily. A female kennel attendant was lying motionless beside the death machine. I knelt and felt for a pulse.

"She's okay. She just fainted."

"Why did she faint?" Amanda said.

"She must have seen this," I said, pointing to the viewing panel on the euthanasia chamber.

Inside the chamber lay the lifeless body of Rhoda Marx.

Chapter 3

From the time I placed the call, it took Sheriff Cassidy ten minutes to arrive at the crime scene. The protestors froze when they heard the sirens and saw the law arrive. They no doubt assumed the shelter had called in a complaint and the police had come to break up the protest; however, there was far worse trouble at the shelter than anyone could have guessed.

Skip's attractive new deputy, Rusty Cannon, had come along to assist him. What is it with Skip and redheads? First that flirty waitress, Rita Ramirez, and now Rusty. From the look on her face, I could tell this was her first murder detail. In this case, green wasn't a good complementary color for red. *Hope you brought barf bags, Skip.*

Rusty had a name like a pole dancer and a figure to match. She filled out every inch of her uniform. Where was Skip doing his recruiting for the force, Vegas? Knowing

Skip, I'm sure he didn't mind having a bodacious crime-scene partner, but right now I had a different kind of body for him to size up.

"What took you so long, Skip? Stop for coffee and Krispy Kremes on the way?"

"Very funny. Where's the stiff?"

"Over there." I pointed toward the euthanasia chamber.

"This is a first. The victim goes to the gas chamber before the killer does." Skip's black brand of humor invariably surfaced at times like these. I was surprised when Rusty didn't laugh at her boss's joke. I would have taken her for the type who would shine up the brass to get ahead in the force. But she seemed more intent on the fact that there was a corpse in the room with us — her first, I surmised as the color drained from her peaches-and-cream complexion. When she clapped a hand to her mouth, I thought she was going to lose it.

"We're not going to need a cleanup on aisle four, are we, Rusty?" Skip said.

She gulped. "No, I'm fine, Chief." Brushing a stray lock of claret hair from her eyes, she slipped on the latex gloves and got down to the unpleasant business at hand. Perhaps I had misjudged Skip's rookie.

"You found her this way?" Skip said to

the still wan-looking kennel attendant who'd had the displeasure of discovering her employer's corpse. She nodded. I could tell he felt empathy for her. He studied her face a few seconds and then glanced down at her name badge, or so it appeared to anyone who doesn't know him as well as I do. Skip is such a pushover for a shapely female. On the other hand, he may have been observing her more as a possible suspect, noting her reaction, her body language, and other behavior.

"Nothing's been touched here. Right, Beanie?"

"Everything's the way we found it."

"I didn't think they still used these contraptions in animal shelters," Skip said as he flipped the latch on the chamber with a gloved hand. When he opened the door, Rhoda's left arm flopped out. It sounded like a wet trout slapping the cold concrete floor. Skip was unperturbed by the sound. He's a veteran fisherman, after all. More than one rainbow trout and Kokanee salmon has met its fate at the end of a hook on one of his many fishing expeditions on the lake in the ol' *Trout Scout.*

"Most don't," I said. "Unfortunately, many municipally funded ones still do."

"We hoped to change over to injection,

but it was too expensive," Amanda said. "There just isn't enough money to do everything you'd like to do."

"Did you know that *euthanasia* means 'good death' in Greek?" Skip liked to make small talk while he was investigating a crime scene, especially if there was a murder victim. It wasn't exactly like whistling while you worked, but the effect was the same. It kept you emotionally detached and allowed you to remain objective. He opened Rhoda's gaping mouth wider. "This definitely wasn't a good death."

"I know," I said. "Death by CO suffocation is cruel, according to the Humane Society of the United States. Sodium pentobarbital is the preferred humane agent for the euthanasia of companion animals."

"Isn't that the same thing they use on death-row inmates?" Rusty asked.

"You're thinking of sodium pentothal, the first of three drugs they administer," Skip said. "It's quick, but some argue it's not painless."

"Who would do something like this?" Amanda said. "I didn't like Rhoda, but she didn't deserve to die like . . . like a dog."

"Some might disagree," I said.

"I don't know who, but it was some dirty dog who had a bone to pick with her," Skip said. "Better secure the crime scene and start lifting some prints off this thing, Rusty."

"Right, Chief."

"Speaking of dogs, I have two waiting for me out in the car," I said. "I'll leave you two to your work. Call me later, Skip? I'll need details for the *Tattler.*"

"Sure thing, Beanie."

As I headed for the car, I heard a canine chorus coming from my Jeep. Cruiser and Calamity were trying to out-howl each other. Cruiser was clearly ready to go home. My new adoptee had no more clue where home was than any of us had about why Rhoda Marx met her end the same way Calamity would have, had I not come in time to rescue her from Lakeside Shelter. How could anyone call such an Auschwitz for animals a shelter, anyway? A shelter should be a *no-kill* facility, and everyone at this murder scene would no doubt have agreed that goes for humans and animals alike.

Chapter 4

Calamity howled all the way over to the vet clinic, and with Cruiser's baying I had surround hound sound. I understood that she was frightened. She had no idea what else lay in store for her, and if she'd known, she wouldn't have been too happy about it. She needed to have a complete checkup before I took her home. She had soiled her cage in transit. I only hoped this mistake was due to anxiety and not one of the diseases that breed at overcrowded shelters like Lakeside.

By the time a dog arrives in a shelter, it's already been through a lot of trauma. It's been separated from its home, its master, and has probably dodged a few speeding cars, as I'm sure Cruiser had before Tom found him. How he managed to survive life on busy Tahoe streets without becoming road kill, I'll never know. I've seen some strays actually wait for traffic lights to change before crossing streets, but basset hounds aren't known for their road sense. Once a hound sets its nose on the trail of its quarry, be it bunny or bagel, he is oblivious to any possible danger he might encounter along the way.

"How's everything looking with Calamity, Doc?" I said.

"She certainly has a good set of teeth." When Doc Heaton gave Calamity the once-over, she'd tried to nip him twice. Once when he poked her fanny with the thermometer and once when he tried to look down her throat. Fortunately, he was accustomed to uncooperative patients and took her attitude in stride. Once he'd nearly lost the tip of his pinky to a testy terrier. There are worse battle scars to bear than those inflicted by a fearful stray in need of medical assistance. At least those were for a good cause.

"I expect you're not the first to discover that," I said.

He laughed. "This little lady's already been spayed, so you won't have to worry about her giving birth to more little piranha pups."

I love a vet with a good sense of humor.

"She looks to be in good shape, but I did a blood panel and took a stool sample to be sure. Hopefully, she doesn't have heartworm or any other parasites. She's definitely underweight for her size, but with some TLC and a good high-protein diet, she should be back to normal in no time. I expect you'll have her all prettied up in time for the Waddle."

"Cruiser and I will take care of that. He won't mind sharing some of his treats with her." Sure he wouldn't. Who was I kidding?

"I think you'd better hold her head while I give her a couple of little jabs here, Elsie. She's a snappish one."

"I hope that won't cause problems in finding her a good home."

"She'll probably settle down after you get her home."

"I expect so. She's been through a lot." I held Calamity close and braced her head firmly so she couldn't do any more damage to Doc Heaton's fingers. A moment later, she was back in her stinky crate. The vet tech had washed it out, but it still reeked. Fortunately, I had a few spares at home. Once back in the car, the doggie duet resumed. Who needs a boom box when you have two bassets howling in the car?

When I veered into the driveway of the old homestead, the howling stopped. Cruiser was only slightly more relieved to be home than I was. I think we both sensed that some challenges lay ahead for us with this newest rescue dog. Calamity was much more high-strung than the other bassets I'd fostered so far. I already knew that much from her behavior in the shelter and in the car. I could only hope she wouldn't live up to her name. In fact, I had to wonder how she got it in the first place. I cut her some slack because I knew she was scared and had most likely suffered some abuse in her past.

She obviously didn't like men, but I didn't live with one, so that wouldn't be a problem. There was just the occasional visit from Skip and Nona's assortment of boyfriends. What would Nona think of her? She was coming up to Tahoe in time for the Waddle. I was glad, not only because I hadn't seen her in a while, but also because I could use an extra pair of hands to help me manage two dogs in a one-dog household.

I opened up the rear door of the Jeep, hefted the sky kennel out and set it down as gently as I could. Calamity's squirming around made it too difficult to carry her in the cage. Besides, it smelled too bad to take in my house. I hesitated to open the cage door, but I had to in order to slip the lead on her. She could have easily slipped my grip, run away, and ended up right back where she started. Like the other unfortunate basset, she probably wouldn't be so lucky a second time. But she didn't try to get away from me. She was just happy to be out of the cage.

The moment she was out of her crate, that nose started sniffing the trees and bushes. I let her have her head, following her around the yard at the end of the leash. Who was leading whom here? Anyone observing us could tell right away. Cruiser made his customary mark on the old piddling pine tree and shot straight to the back porch. I heard the flap of the dog door and knew I had one less dog to worry about for the moment. I knew he would make a beeline for his raining cats and dogs quilt at the end of my bed. He was already claiming his territory, in case the newcomer might have any confusion as to who was top dog around the MacBean house.

After Calamity had finished her sniff and squat tour of the backyard and rechristened Cruiser's pine tree, I led her inside. She seemed calm enough, so I decided to let her off the leash to explore her new surroundings. I realize only in retrospect that this was my first mistake with Calamity. It was important for her to feel comfortable in my home, but I shouldn't have given her free reign yet. I was accustomed to calmer hounds like my easygoing couch spud, Cruiser. Once released, she hurtled through the house, looking for the quickest way out. I dashed over to Cruiser's dog door, flipped down the security panel and locked it in the nick of time before Calamity found her escape hatch.

Perhaps it was the scent of Cruiser and the lingering aura of other rescued dogs that set off her full-scale panic attack. Or maybe she was looking for her other master or perhaps a sibling or two. Who knows what was going through that pointy little noggin of hers? When she saw there was no escape, she flopped down on her haunches and began to bay mournfully.

To my dog-loving ears, hearing her howl that way was like hearing a lost child crying for its mother, and perhaps that's exactly what it was. I had no doubt she was a puppy mill dog that had been separated from her mother at six weeks of age or even younger. How could anyone at the shelter have expected her to be socialized when all she'd probably ever known in her life was the inside of a cage? Her lament tore at my heart like a pup with an old leather slipper. Only another basset could manage to look any more pitiful than Calamity did at that moment. I tried to soothe her, to distract her with another treat, but it did no good. She wasn't having any of it.

Cruiser came running from my bedroom to see what was the matter. When Calamity saw him coming toward her, she took off in the opposite direction. Thinking this was an invitation to play, Cruiser chased after her, barking and baying his excitement, which only made things worse. Each time they rounded the table, I tried to intercept Calamity or Cruiser, with no success. Between the two of them they upset my furniture and knocked over lamps and broke a couple of vases. By the time I could lasso her again with the leash, the whole place looked like the result of a smash-and-grab home invasion robbery. What had I gotten myself into with this nutty dog?

Exhausted, I sat down on Tom's chair to catch my breath after the doggy decathlon in my living room. The dogs had finally worn themselves down. Cruiser climbed up on the couch and perched on his hair-coated pillow.

"Sit, Calamity!" She had no idea what that command meant, but she was so pooped from the chase she sat anyway. About the time everyone was all settled down, the phone rang. Calamity shot up like she'd gotten another needle jab from Doc Heaton.

"Easy, girl. It's only the telephone." She leapt onto the ottoman, in case Cruiser decided to start chasing her again.

"Hi, Mom. It's me."

"H . . . hi, Nona."

"You sound out of breath. Been out exercising with Cruiser on the mountain trails again?"

"No, I was doing a little indoor exercising with Cruiser and Calamity."

"Calamity? Don't tell me you've taken in another basset boarder."

"Yes, and I think this one's going to live up to her name." I sighed as I surveyed the wreckage in the living room.

"A female this time?"

"Yep."

"That should make Cruiser a happy camper."

"Not thus far. Besides, he's neutered and she's spayed. What's he gonna do?"

Nona laughed.

"You coming up for the Waddle?"

"That's why I was calling you. I'm taking some vacation time. I wanted to be sure you don't mind putting up with me for a while."

"Are you kidding? The question is, will you be able to put up with us?"

Nona's laugh sounded melodic to my ears.

As light as wind in aspen trees. "Don't I always?"

"When are you coming?"

"I'll be up late tomorrow."

"No boyfriends tagging along?" Neither of us had forgotten Medwyn's visit one deadly winter.

"Don't sweat it, Mom. It'll be just me this time. Sounds like you have your hands full enough there with Cruiser and Calamity."

I didn't mention the other business at the shelter over the phone. Nona would find out about it soon enough. It would be good to have my lovely daughter here with me again, at least for a little while. She was so busy these days with her modeling career, which often took her abroad, it seemed she came to visit less and less. In years past, she'd spent all her time swimming in the lake, or water skiing on it, and flirting with the beautiful boys of summer. No matter how far away she journeyed, Nona would always return to Tahoe each summer as our Washoe ancestors did.

Since her father had passed away, I was grateful for her company, even if it was only the occasional visit. She is the only family I have left other than Cruiser. Like him, Nona is always there for me, no matter what kind of *calamity* her mother gets mixed up with.

Chapter 5

The dogs had finally calmed down, and I started cleaning up the mess they'd made of my house in their mad dash around the place. Fortunately, they'd only broken an inexpensive vase and not any of the priceless Washoe artifacts I keep displayed on shelves in my living room. Good thing bassets are too short to reach very high up, but those long, perpetual-motion tails can do some damage if you're not careful. I keep most of my valuables above tail-wagging level. It's also a good thing Tom left me a little nest egg and the *Tattler* keeps me busy writing articles. At this rate, rescuing rascally hounds could get expensive.

Calamity had conked out on Tom's old ottoman. Her long, long ears enveloped her like a silken blanket. I suspected she was either worn out from the morning's events or she was having a mild reaction to the vaccinations Doc Heaton gave her. I'd seen

Cruiser go through this before with his booster shots. Watching her curled up there reminded me of the night Tom arrived on our doorstep with a thin, forlorn-looking stray hound dog. I remembered Cruiser lying on Tom's lap that night and two pairs of sad eyes staring at me with a look that said, "Can I please keep him?" I was powerless to refuse, and I've been a pushover for basset hounds ever since, even when they were the ones doing the pushing over, as they'd done to my furniture during Calamity's calamitous homecoming.

I righted the upset lamp and then busied myself scooping up shards of broken glass. I feared I might be scooping much more than this after my new adoptee had finished adjusting to her new abode. I didn't even know whether she was house-trained. She'd already had one accident in the car on the way home. *Just tackle one problem at a time, Beanie.*

As I headed to the front closet for the broom, I spotted Skip striding up to my porch. I met him at the door before he could ring the doorbell and get the dogs all riled up again.

"Hi, Beanie. What happened in here? A home invasion?"

"You could say that."

The moment Calamity heard Skip's voice she barked her alarm, launched from the ottoman, and shot down the hallway. I didn't have the energy to chase after her again, so I let her go. Things could have been worse; at least she wasn't attacking my houseguest. It was clear to me by now that she had some serious issues with men. Cruiser, on the other hand, looked up, saw it was Skip, thumped his tail twice on the sofa, then went back to snoring and his dream of chasing rabbits in an alpine meadow.

"At least one dog here is happy to see me. Sort of."

"Don't mind Cruiser. Our new houseguest wore him out. It's been a stressful morning for all of us."

"You can say that again." Skip sat down next to Cruiser and stroked his head. I was glad Cruiser still had a male influence in his life. It was clear that despite the slobber, Skip didn't mind being his step dog-dad. Cruiser grunted his pleasure at the attention he was getting and rested his chin on Skip's knee for better stroking advantage.

"Finished up at the shelter, Skip?"

"Yeah, this was my first experience with euthanasia."

"Lucky you," I said. "I only wish it was

the same for Lakeside Shelter. I agree with TAILS. Lakeside doesn't deserve to be called a shelter. They destroy far more animals than they place in homes, and the rest go to research labs. A shelter should be a no-kill facility. Period!"

"You can never call it that now. Not after today."

"That's for doggone sure." Skip may have his black humor as a release valve for defusing tense situations, but I have my canine quips.

"So, any ideas who might have had a grudge against Rhoda Marx?"

"You mean besides every animal lover in Tahoe?"

"Made a few enemies along the way, huh?"

"Yeah, thanks in part to the *Tattler* and a certain reporter who shall remain nameless."

"I guess it kind of goes with that line of work. Nobody loves the dogcatcher."

"It's a hard job, I'm sure. I couldn't do it, that's for certain. It's tough enough going down there to rescue the dogs. If I worked there, I'd end up with my own animal shelter full of stray dogs and cats. Not to mention the bunnies that get dumped after Easter."

"I'm sure Cruiser would love for you to adopt bunnies. He's not allergic to them like I am."

"I didn't know you were allergic to bunnies, Skip. Does this mean you've cancelled your subscription to *Playboy*?"

When Skip blushed, his freckles were like seeds on a strawberry. Embarrassed, he quickly changed the subject. "People who work in shelters get a bad rap sometimes, kind of like peace officers do. We're just doing our jobs, after all."

"Yeah, nobody likes the dogcatcher, but they're only cleaning up the mess left by folks who don't spay and neuter their pets or who buy pets on a whim without considering the responsibility that goes with caring for one. Sometimes the rap is well deserved, though, as in Marx's case. She's handled things badly with the public, shelter personnel, and especially rescue groups, and the animals have paid for her mistakes."

"So did she." As Skip talked, Cruiser turned belly up for a tummy rub. No point in wasting an opportunity for a full body massage.

For some reason, the talk of Playboy bunnies brought Skip's new partner to mind. "How'd Rusty do at the crime scene this morning?"

"I don't know. I'm still trying to decide."

"What do you mean?"

"We had a disagreement about proper procedure, and I had to step in and take over. She didn't appreciate being dressed down on the job."

"That's too bad." I felt immediate empathy for Rusty. I'd had bosses who did the same thing and made me feel foolish in front of my peers. "Couldn't you have talked to her about it later?"

"If a rookie is doing something wrong, I can't let her foul up evidence. She needs to learn to check her ego at the door when we enter a crime scene."

"I suppose you're right. What was the problem, though?"

"At first I thought she was missing evidence, but she insisted she'd done it correctly. I guess she was, because when I dusted the chamber for prints, I got the same result."

"What?"

"We found those of Rhoda Marx and a couple of other shelter personnel."

"That's not surprising. They work there and have probably operated the machine."

"I know that, but there were other prints we couldn't explain."

"What prints?"

Skip had a funny look on his face, and at first I thought he was jerking my choke chain when he said, "We found dog prints."

"What other kinds of prints would you expect to find at an animal shelter?"

"The thing is, the prints weren't inside the thing. We found paw prints on the outside, even on the door handle."

"I'm not sure what you're suggesting."

"Neither am I. Perhaps we'll know more when the full report is in and we've been able to question some of the shelter staff more thoroughly. Rusty is signed up for a training class for the next couple of weeks."

"Sending her back to rookie school already?"

He laughed. "No, it's one of those employee relations things they make us all attend to keep Internal Affairs happy. I was hoping maybe you can help me out a bit in her absence, if your busy writing schedule allows."

"Sure. Actually, it should fit right in with my busy writing schedule. I have to keep Carla at the *Tattler* happy, too. Let me know the medical examiner's findings on Rhoda when you get them, will you?"

"Will do. I expect his report should be on my desk soon. Hope so, anyway. The caseload has been getting backed up lately with all the summer drug activity."

"I've never understood why people would

need drugs at Tahoe. This scenic place is all the drug anyone could ever need."

"What was that stuff your grandpa used to smoke in that ceremonial pipe of his?"

"Watch it, paleface. I'll have to sic our tribal watchdogs on you."

"Please, these two watchdogs are enough for me. Besides, I suppose everyone has to have his drug of choice. As for me, I'll take caffeine."

"I'll brew us a fresh pot of coffee if you like."

"Don't bother. I really should be getting back. I'll grab some java on the way back to the office."

"You're going to leave me here with this vicious beast? Some public protector you are, Skip."

Skip laughed. "Don't forget you have your trusty sidekick, Cruiser. He's been known to back you up in a tight spot from time to time. And now you have Calamity, too."

"Yeah, double trouble." I wasn't sure if Cruiser was going to be much help to me in taming the little four-legged, long-eared shrew I'd rescued. Like Skip, Cruiser is a pushover for a pretty face.

"This is quite a mess you have here to clean up," Skip said, surveying my disheveled room. "Are you sure you haven't gotten in over your head with this new dog of yours?"

"Could be." Skip is a master at stating the obvious, but what he had told me about the evidence surrounding the death of Rhoda Marx promised to be an even bigger mess to clean up. "I need to get this place tidied up before Calamity makes another one. Besides, Nona's coming up soon for a visit, and I don't want the place looking like a wreck."

"Whew, it's a wreck all right, I've seen tidier smash and grabs."

A smash from the back bedroom accented Skip's words as though he'd cued the action.

"What was that?" Skip instinctively slapped his holster, ready to draw his weapon.

"Calamity!" I yelped, dashing down the hallway with Skip and Cruiser hot on my heels.

CHAPTER 6

"It's a smash and grab, for sure," I said when I saw the basket I'd painstakingly assembled for the Waddle overturned on the floor. The perpetrator was still at the scene of the crime, gutting the basket of its yummy contents. Calamity had torn open the bags of carob-chip cookies, gobbled them down and was proceeding to rip apart the one filled with Cruiser's favorite, Bacon Beggin' Strips. And in case any canine crime scene investigator might wonder who had perpetrated the deed, her carob-coated muzzle was evidence enough of having committed the offense. "Caught in the act, Calamity!"

"I see now why you named her that."

"I didn't. She came with the name."

"It's perfect for this dog." Skip eyed this scene in the same way he assesses any other crime scene, including the one he encountered at the shelter, noting every minute detail. Was he going to dust for paw prints here, too? I halfway expected him to pull out his handcuffs and read Calamity her rights.

"That's really all I know about her, though. I have absolutely no information about her health history or where she came from, but from what I've seen thus far, I suspect she's probably damaged goods. She may have been abused in her former home. I think I really have my work cut out for me."

"How could anyone ever think of mistreating a basset hound? I mean, get a load of that innocent face."

"I suspect you'll find a pair of devil horns poking up beneath that hound halo of hers."

Despite visible evidence to the contrary, Calamity was the picture of innocence, all right, but I knew from past experience that inside the head of the basset is a cunning mind that will stop at nothing to obtain the desired objective, which is usually food. I had no doubt she was plotting her next domestic exploit as we spoke.

"I can't imagine how a beautiful dog like this could end up dumped at a shelter."

"It happens more often than you'd care to know, Skip. Mostly, people can't deal with that hound stubborn streak. Bassets are single-minded when in the pursuit of a scent trail."

"Like pursuit of a stash of treats, you mean."

"I'll say! It does make them a bit harder to train than some breeds, and folks too frequently mistake a basset's stubbornness for stupidity. Some don't like their howling, either. It's not music to everyone's ears like it is to mine." When I reached for the Beggin' Strips, my gesture was met with a warning growl.

"Careful, Beanie. I think she means to keep her prize."

"Uh-oh. Looks like we have some food-guarding issues, too." In spite of Calamity's threats, I called her bluff and managed to nab the last bit of evidence away from her before she ingested it bag and all, with a finger or two for dessert. I didn't need more vet bills for an attack of pancreatitis.

"It's my fault. I shouldn't have left the basket within easy reach. She's probably starved. I should have offered her some kibble right away when I brought her home, but I got distracted."

"She does look a little underfed."

"I know. She's underweight for her size, so she's not been getting enough food. Someone probably dumped the poor girl in the backyard and forgot about her. It's going to take a little creativity at mealtimes, though. I have two dogs with different dietary needs, and I can't keep kibble available for Cruiser all the time or he'll inflate like a zeppelin."

"He's sure come a long way from when you first got him."

"Amazing what a little TLC can do, isn't it? After a few weeks with us, he was a different dog. He looked more like Calamity does now when he first came here. I hope I can work the same magic with this dog. It's going to take more than a new diet, I think, to make a new dog out of *her.*"

"I'll leave you two to your tug of war. I have a mounting caseload waiting for me back at the office and a new deputy to break in. As if I really needed a murder investigation on top of it all. And I think this one is going to be a real dog."

"I suppose that's to be expected with a murder at the dog pound."

Chapter 7

Mealtimes at the MacBean house kennel had suddenly become more complicated, as I discovered on the morning following Calamity's arrival. Now there were two mouths to feed different canine cuisine. Cruiser and I were on a low-cal diet, but my anorexic adoptee needed a dietary regimen to help her quickly put on weight and get prettied up for possible adoption at the Waddle. Judging from the raffle basket incident, she wasn't a picky eater. Is there any such thing in Bassetdom? If there was, I hadn't yet encountered one.

All I had at the house was Cruiser's diet kibble to feed her that morning, which she gobbled with gusto, but I'd have to pay a visit to the pet store to pick up some special food for my new boarder. I decided to leave the dogs behind this time, but I couldn't trust Calamity not to get into trouble again. I tried to coax her into the crate, but she wasn't having anything further to do with cages of any kind. After her experience at the shelter, I can't say I blamed her. So I left her locked in the spare bedroom. Only this time I made sure there was nothing else she could get in to.

The moment I led her into the room and shut the door behind me, she began barking her head off. Calamity's bark was nothing like Cruiser's, which was deep, melodious, and pleasant to the ear. Hers was a sharp, hysterical yelp. *Oh, great,* I thought. *Separation anxiety, too.* This dog was a furry funhouse of troubles. I assumed that she'd settle down after I left. I was so wrong. I could still hear her yapping as I backed out of the drive and drove down the street. Poor Cruiser. He wouldn't be getting any sleep while I was gone.

Sally Applebaum, the owner of the Haute Hydrant, is active in all the local pet causes, including Found Hounds. She was donating a lot of merchandise to our upcoming fundraiser and would be providing numerous raffle items, including dog beds, coats and sweaters and, of course, plenty of treats. Sally is a whole lot of woman with a supersized heart to match.

"Hello, Beanie!" Sally chirped her usual friendly greeting as I entered the shop. Summer roses flowered on her full cheeks when she smiled. Fabian, Sally's adored Yorkie and official store Welcome Waggin', trotted over to me and sniffed the bouquet of basset on my pants leg. He recognized Cruiser's scent from past visits to the store, but the new Eau de Calamity made him linger a bit longer than usual.

"Hi, Sally. How's the pet biz?"

"It's been quieter than usual, but then Sundays are always a bit slow." I knew Sally was being her cheery, optimistic self, although a little positive thinking never hurts in hard times. The economic slump hit small shops like hers hard. Less money in people's pockets meant less money to spend on their pets, and the Haute Hydrant wasn't the only one in Tahoe feeling the crunch. Even chain stores like the new Petropolis on the North Shore were tightening their collars a few notches to make ends meet. "Need more diet kibble already for that chow hound of yours?"

"No, he's got plenty of that. I need to add some weight, not take it away."

"I know you don't mean Cruiser, so I'm guessing you must have taken in another foster." Sally motioned for me to come with her. I followed her to the aisle where she kept the dog food. There were so many brands to choose from, I'd have never been able to make a choice as quickly as she could. Sally knows more bits about kibble than anyone. I trusted that she'd pick the perfect nutritional food for my new foster dog. I didn't want to stay away too long, in case Calamity was getting into any more mischief in my absence.

"Yep. This one's going to be a handful, I can tell. It's no wonder that no one had adopted her yet at Lakeside Animal Shelter."

"It's a wonder anyone ever adopts a pet from that place. And they don't give people half a chance to adopt the ones that are adoptable."

"I always thought they held them a couple of weeks."

"Most people assume that, and they don't want the public to know the truth. Much of the time animals are destroyed before they can even be evaluated and put up for adoption."

"I had no idea."

"Some animals are only in there for a few hours. No one even has a chance to see them. Small dogs and purebreds stand a better chance of adoption, but bully breeds are dead on arrival. No one adopts the pits and Rotties. Cats stand hardly any chance at all."

"That's a crying shame, Sally."

"Sure is. Something has got to change. There are too many pets coming in, too little space, and too few personnel. That's why volunteers are so important, but they can't even keep volunteers there for long. Not now, anyway."

"Why is that?"

"Things changed for the worse after that horrid Marx woman came on board as manager. She's a cold one."

"You can say that again." Sally didn't know just how cold Rhoda was now.

"If you dare to offer a dissenting opinion, Medusa Marx can turn you to stone with a glance. I volunteered there for years, but finally I couldn't take it anymore. From what I hear, things haven't improved any since I left. In fact, they even have a hard time keeping paid employees on the staff for more than a few months at a time. I don't know how people can stand to work there day in and day out and see what goes on behind closed doors. It's a disgrace."

"Things are even worse there now."

"What do you mean?"

"Someone died."

"What happened? Don't tell me someone

finally gave Rhoda Marx her comeuppance?"

"That's exactly what I'm telling you. Her death is being investigated as a homicide. How did you know the victim was Rhoda Marx? It hasn't even been reported in the papers yet."

"Lucky guess. Everyone who ever worked with Rhoda hated her like poison."

"Sounds like you didn't like her much, either." It took me by surprise to hear my friend even utter the word *hate.* It was so un-Sally-like.

"I'm just saying that she could be very unpleasant when she wanted to be, which was most of the time, according to her co-workers. I once saw her reduce one of her female employees to tears, then say to her, 'I'll have no crybabies on my staff.' "

"Who was that?"

"Can't recall. She left the shelter shortly afterward."

"I'm sure there are disgruntled employees in every office, but who would hate Rhoda enough to want to kill her?"

Sally didn't look up from the cash register as she punched in the price code for my bag of Wholesome Hound kibble. "Who wouldn't?"

Chapter 8

As I drove back to the cabin, Sally Applebaum's comments roiled in my brain like the summer storm clouds on the horizon. The cool breeze wafting through my car window had grown cold and, like Sally's words, sent a chill clattering up my spine like a row of kennel doors clanging shut. I had seen a dark side of my friend, who for as long as I'd known her had always kept her sunny side up.

Perhaps her uncharacteristic negativity was also a symptom of our troubled times. Too many people. Too little money. Too much traffic, noise, and pollution. Too many animals and not enough homes for them all. But no one ever expects things to turn deadly, even when they do.

Seeing Nona's bright yellow Volkswagen beetle parked in my driveway scattered my depressing thoughts like the V of geese fleeing the gathering storm. Hooray! Nona was here! Things would be better now. Like Cruiser, I am always happier when the pack at the MacBean house is complete.

The first drops of rain drummed a lively tattoo on the car roof as I hefted from the car the bag of dog chow and other goodies I'd bought at the Haute Hydrant.

"Need any help with that, Mom?"

"No, thanks, honey. I've got it."

"Better hurry, it's starting to rain."

"Coming!" I made it to the front door as the first rumbles of thunder volleyed overhead and the heavens opened up. I could think of nothing better than Nona and me chatting over some hot tea during a summer storm. We had some catching up to do, but first things first. Some introductions were in order. I only hoped Calamity would be more congenial to Nona than she'd been to Skip.

"Come give your mom a big hug, Papoose."

Nona and I gave each other bear hugs. She felt like a sparrow in my arms.

"Have you given up eating altogether? You can carry that skinny model stuff too far, you know."

"It's hard finding time to eat on my crazy schedule."

"Well, you've got some time off now, so

I'll put some meat on those bones while you're here."

When Nona didn't reply, I knew I was in danger of crossing the badger barrier, so I changed the subject. I didn't want to chase her off the moment she arrived. This time I wanted her here for a good, long stay.

"How was your drive up the hill?"

"Fine, except for the usual traffic hang-up at Placerville."

"Why do you think they called it Hang-town? Have you already met Cruiser's and my new roomie?"

"Yeah. She was shrieking like a teakettle when I got here. She calmed down after I let her out of the back room, though."

"Oh, no! You let her out? And she didn't tear the place apart?"

"No, she's fine now. I gave her the rest of the sandwich I had left over from lunch. She wolfed it down, then fell sound asleep."

"Where is she?"

"She's lying on your bed, where Cruiser usually sleeps."

"Uh-oh. His Lordship may not take too kindly to that. I expect I'll have to come up with other sleeping arrangements while she's staying here."

"Speaking of teakettles, how about brewing us some tea, Mom?"

"Sure, as soon as I restock the pup pantry. Earl Grey okay?"

"Perfect."

I stashed Calamity's kibble beside Cruiser's low-cal variety in the Yum-Yum Nook. You can always tell when you're in the home of a dog lover. There's more food and treats stored in the larder for the pets than for the people. My pantry resembled the shelves at the Haute Hydrant. The bottom shelf held a variety of canned food in nearly every flavor, from trout to turducken, to appease Cruiser's discriminating palate. On the second shelf I kept all the sundry canine remedies: ear washes, sprays, ointments, pills and such. And on the top shelf, out of basset-raiding range, were the treats.

So far, Cruiser hadn't discovered how to use a chair to reach the uppermost shelf, although I've heard of bassets that have. One dog pushed a chair up to the kitchen counter one Christmas, climbed atop it, and not only demolished a standing prime rib roast but also tossed holiday hors d'oeuvres onto the floor for the rest of his low-slung cohorts in crime.

Satisfied that everything was stashed safely away, I brewed some tea for Nona and me. By the time the kettle whistle shrieked, arrows of rain pelted the kitchen window. I flicked on the kitchen light when the storm's full fury blackened the skies to obsidian.

I handed Nona her special cup with the cross-country skiers on it. "Here's your tea, dear."

"Thanks." She took a long, slow sip and smiled at me. I noticed that her gingersnap eyes didn't have quite the same spice to them as I remembered. "I'm so glad you were able to find another cup like the one that broke. I loved that cup."

"I know. You'd had it since you were a child. Your grandma let you use it when we used to come up and visit. That's why I tried so hard to search for another cup just like it. Finally found one at a thrift shop."

"Gosh, it feels good to be here again. Sitting down with you over tea and chatting about old times is so comforting."

"I'm glad you're here. It gets pretty lonely here sometimes without you."

"If only Dad were here too, everything would be perfect, like it was before . . ." Nona's eyes misted. "I sure do miss him sometimes."

"Me too, honey. I still expect to see him sitting in that old easy chair reading his paper, or sometimes, when Cruiser barks and runs to the door, I think it must be your father coming home for supper, but of course, it never is. Usually, it's Skip, which is almost as good in Cruiser's estimation."

"He loves Skip nearly as much as he did Dad."

"I know. That's why I keep him around." I laughed.

"Who? Cruiser or Skip? They're both your partners in crime."

Nona didn't know the half of it.

"You might as well tell me what's going on, Mother. I'll read all about it in the *Tattler,* anyway." There was no fooling Nona. She could read her mom like a dog-eared book. "Please don't tell me you're mixed up in another murder investigation."

"All right. I won't tell you."

"Be serious. You know I'll ask Skip if you won't tell me."

"If you want to play Truth or Dare, Nona, I'm game. I'll tell you the truth about what's going on in my life, but I dare you to tell me the same about your own." There's more than one way to nose into my daughter's life.

Nona picked up her cup of tea and took another sip before answering. "Okay, but you first."

I took a few sips of my cooling Earl Grey before our mother-daughter powwow commenced. For several minutes the room was silent except for the steady drumbeat of rain on the roof and the click of toenails on linoleum. One way or the other, calamity was about to befall me.

Chapter 9

I was actually relieved when Calamity charged into the kitchen, looking for more trouble to get into. She was a welcome distraction because I knew Nona wasn't going to like what I was about to tell her. Namely, how another newspaper assignment for the *Tattler* had gotten her mother involved in much more than researching and typing an article. I know she worries about me almost as much as I worry about her when we're apart.

Before I could stop her, Calamity made a beeline for Cruiser's Yum-Yum Nook. I had left the door ajar and her keen nose led her straight to the third shelf, the treat treasure trove. Far more agile than Cruiser, she stretched her full length, easily reaching the bag of Bacon Beggin' Strips she'd ripped open before.

"Oh no you don't!" I intercepted the bag mid-snatch as she snapped at empty air. I held the bag high over my head, shifting it from hand to hand as she leapt repeatedly to gain the prize. For a moment we must have looked like a pair of basketball players scuffling there in the pantry, with me guarding the home cupboard advantage. Only when I dropped the ball, or in this case, treat, did she retreat from her offense. Game won, Calamity trotted off with her bacon strip.

Exhausted, I flopped down in my chair. "Now, where were we? Oh, yes . . ."

Nona listened without comment while I told her about my activities at the shelter and the discovery of Rhoda Marx's body. I think Nona is secretly proud of her mom's reputation in Tahoe as not only a stringer for a newspaper but a respected and intuitive crime-solver.

"All right, Nona, I've told you everything. Now it's your turn. So spill." My mind raced faster than the wind in the pines outside my cabin as I wondered what my daughter was about to tell me. Was it a new boyfriend? Was she dating a nice man this time? Could she even be getting engaged to be married? Then my mind wrapped around all the negative possibilities. Was she finally migrating across a vast ocean to Europe to pursue her blossoming career as a supermodel? Was she pregnant? Nothing I imagined could have prepared me for what my only daughter was about to say.

"I found a lump, Mom."

A lump clotted in my throat at the mere mention of the word. Finally, I managed to squeak out, "A lump? Where?"

"Right here." There was a lump all right. It felt about the size of a pea.

"Did you have a mammogram?"

"Yes. And an ultrasound, too. Inconclusive. Next up is a biopsy."

"When?"

"I was supposed to go next week, but I decided to come up here instead. I wanted to talk to you about it first, Mom."

Nona rarely asked for my advice in her life decisions. I was honored that she was asking now; I only wished it had been about anything but this. I hadn't known how to respond when my own mother had told me she had cancer. All I could recall about that terrible moment, still frozen in my memory, was feeling like I'd been trampled by a herd of buffalo. I felt the same way now.

Neither of us dared utter the "C" word, but it hovered in the room with us like the blackest thundercloud.

"Try not to worry. It might be nothing, dear. Not all lumps are malignant. False-positive mammograms are pretty common. You've been under a lot of stress with your career. It could just be a clogged gland or a cyst." I knew even as I said it that I was trying harder to convince myself than her that everything was okay.

"You're probably right." The furrows of worry in Nona's brow could have rivaled a basset hound's.

"Maybe you should have gone ahead and had the biopsy, to be certain. At least you'd know one way or the other. It's best not to delay too long with these things."

"I know I probably should have, and the doctors were pressuring me to have it done. I guess I'm afraid of what they might tell me. If it is malignant, I'm not sure what course I would pursue. White man's medicine is bad. You've said it yourself."

"I know." I remembered how my mother had suffered toward the end of her illness. The standard slash, burn, poison method of cancer treatment hadn't worked for her. The cancer returned despite every painful, invasive procedure the doctors subjected her to. Only when in desperation we turned to the old ways was she able to find any relief from her affliction and live out what time she had relatively pain-free. Her final days had been spent peacefully in her own home surrounded by the familiar things of her life and her loved ones, instead of at a cancer clinic undergoing endless grueling treatments. But Nona was young, too young to be diagnosed with cancer.

"I want to see a tribal doctor, Mother. Can you arrange it for me?"

"Of course, honey." Naturally, I understood that this meant I'd have to seek help from my old rival, Sonseah Little Feather, but I'd do it — for Nona's sake.

CHAPTER 10

It wasn't only the sultry summer storm that kept me awake that night, tossing and turning until I was wrapped in a cocoon of covers. Poor Cruiser grunted his displeasure about having to shift his position every time I did. My mind raced with worry. If thoughts about what Nona had told me weren't enough to keep me wide awake, there was always my restless rescue and an unsolved murder.

At bedtime, I had to dose Calamity with some Rescue Remedy because the thunderstorm was freaking her out. She shivered and shook with fear until the herbal cocktail began to take effect. I began to wonder how many more issues came in this little basset basket case. Perhaps I'd take a dose of the stuff myself, since it also works to soothe stressed-out humans. I tried coaxing Calamity into her crate, first with a Beggin' Strip, a spoonful of peanut butter, even a sample of imported cheese. It was useless. She refused to set one paw inside it. I knew it wouldn't work to have her sleep with Cruiser at the foot of my bed. He wouldn't stand for it. Besides, with two big basset hounds stretched across the bed, where would I sleep?

I understood that she was disoriented and confused. After being shuffled around so much in her short life, how could she possibly know where home was, or even *what* home was? People have no conception of the harm they inflict on these sensitive, domesticated creatures when they tire of the puppy they got for Christmas or the one they fell for in the pet store window, then toss them aside like yesterday's broken toys. By the time a dog has spent time chained in the backyard and ultimately surrendered and impounded, they truly are broken, in body and spirit.

I prepared a bed on the floor in my room for Calamity and she stayed there, for a little while. Next thing I knew there was a cold nose nudging my hand. Apparently, not even natural herbs were a sure remedy to completely soothe her nerves tonight. Or mine.

"Go lie down, Calamity!" She did, for a little while. Then she began exploring the bedroom for something to get into. I heard the rustle of paper and knew she'd found the trashcan. I led her over to her bed and stroked her, talking softly, trying to get her calmed down and more relaxed in her surroundings.

"Now, stay. Go to sleep, girl." She obeyed my command until I had slid under the covers, then she was up like a shot, nosing into something else. I began to think I was fostering a ferret. She was certainly more nocturnal than Cruiser, who was snoring blissfully on his quilt at the foot of the bed. Even when a volley of thunder crashed, he never flicked an eyelash. Calamity, on the other hand, was terrified. I managed to calm her down again, but when she wouldn't stay in her bed, in desperation I took her bedding out to the living room and got her settled out there. I went back to bed and shut the door. It was quiet, at least for a moment or two. I had just closed my eyes when I heard her scratching and whining at my door.

"No!" I repeated it once or twice and then I heard nothing more from her. With the house finally silent, I soon slipped off to sleep, snoring in concert with Cruiser . . .

My mother and I were hiking up the trail together behind the cabin, as we often did when she was alive. Night blanketed the mountain as we headed for a tribal gathering. Mom held my hand, as she had from the time I was a child, guiding me, leading me, always in the direction I should go in life. Cruiser was there too, trudging along beside us while sniffing and marking the wild scents among the scrub.

Somewhere along the trail, Nona emerged from the pines and joined us. She wore the ceremonial costume young girls of our tribe are dressed in when they die. Her pristine white buckskin dress shimmered like a ghost in the moonlight. She clutched a shield of beautiful Washoe basketwork to her breast. We climbed to the crest of the mountain, where a bonfire was blazing. The glow could be seen from a great distance. Then I heard coming from far off the criers, women who moaned and cried night and day for the dead. Their mournful wails echoed through the forest.

When we arrived at the campfire, Nona handed the basket to me. It was the finest of basketry, expertly woven, like the baskets of Dat-so-la-lee, whose work is still prized for its intricacy and beauty. My mother and I filled the basket with healing, medicinal plants, and then handed it back to Nona. She set it on a rock beside the fire and the three of us danced around the fire while the singers grunted, as the Washoe call the singing on such tribal occasions.

The wailing of the women grew louder and louder, then suddenly it was not women I heard crying but a cacophony of dogs howling. It seemed like I was at Lakeside Shelter, walking down the aisle that led to the euthanasia chamber. Every dog in the place was howling and yapping. Something was terribly wrong, but what was it? What were they trying to tell me? In my dream and even when I awoke drenched in sweat, my heart thudding in my breast like a drumbeat, I understood that this was a warning of danger.

Chapter 11

Morning came too quickly. My bloodshot eyes matched Cruiser's. Drooping red haws, typical of the basset hound, always make him look like someone's been spiking his water bowl. Spending a restless night in my bed with me doing a war dance sure hadn't helped matters any.

"Come on, boy. Time to rise and shine." Cruiser groaned his displeasure at my wakeup call and eased off the edge of the bed. Suddenly, I remembered that there were now two hounds in the house. Where was the other one? Oh, yeah. I'd locked her out of the bedroom so Cruiser and I could get some sleep. Heaven only knew what she'd gotten into in the rest of the house during the night. I was afraid to find out, but I opened the bedroom door, ready to face the damage. No Calamity. Cruiser ambled past me toward the kitchen to seek out the next most important thing in his world besides sleep . . . food.

I followed my hungry hound down the hall and into the living room but found neither hide nor hair of Calamity. Had I forgotten to lock Cruiser's dog door after he went out at bedtime? If so, my new foster was no doubt long gone, and the way I was feeling this morning I wasn't sure I'd have been too broken-hearted about it. It's not that I minded having more than four paws pattering around the place. I've had several dogs at once before, and I say the more the merrier, and the hairier. What does it matter that furballs the size of Sasquatch lurk in every corner of my house? That's the price of puppy love. Nonetheless, I had to admit that this dog was far more of a challenge than I was accustomed to. Cruiser had blended right into our lives as though he'd always lived here. Not so, Calamity.

The dog door was secured, so I felt assured that she hadn't escaped. I crept back down the hall and peeked in the open door of the guest bedroom where Nona slept whenever she visited. She was turned away from me, facing the mirrored closet door. Her luxuriant chestnut hair draped the pillow like a red satin ribbon. I could see in the reflection that she was still sound asleep. No sign of my adoptee, though, or at least that's what I thought until I glimpsed two russet heads instead of one poking out from under the duvet. Calamity was tucked under the covers right beside Nona with her pointy noggin resting on the fluffy feather pillow like a princess. When I clucked my tongue in amusement, and mild exasperation at the drool I was sure to find caked on my brand new duvet, a shiny black nose popped out from under the covers. Calamity reared up and cast me a coy backward glance, no doubt gloating at me for having succeeded in worming her way into someone else's warm bed for the night.

I tried without success to coax her out of the bed without waking Nona. I beckoned in a whisper, "Calamity, come," but she wasn't about to budge an inch from her cozy cocoon. I couldn't really blame her. She'd probably known little enough comfort thus far in her young life, so I wasn't about to deny her that for the sake of a washable bedspread.

I had resigned myself to let them both sleep undisturbed when the phone jangled an alarm. I hurried to snatch it from the cradle before it rang again. I knew Nona needed her beauty rest, and Calamity, too.

"Hello?"

"Hi, Elsie, it's Jenna. I just got a frantic

call from Amanda Peabody at the shelter."

"What's wrong?"

"She says someone broke into the shelter last night. All the dogs are gone!"

"Gone? How strange. Any idea who might have done this?"

"She's pretty sure it's the TAILS activists."

"Seems likely, since they've been threatening to take action if conditions at the shelter don't improve. What can I do to help?"

"See if you can find out for sure who's behind this, and if you should see any strays running loose around town, let me know right away. We'll take them in, and I'll try to get them fostered instead of letting the dogcatcher take them back to the shelter."

"How many fugitives are we looking for?"

"A couple dozen. I'll get descriptions of the dogs from Amanda. She'll help us out as much as she can. She's been working on building an adoption Web site to find homes for strays."

"Okay, I'll keep an eye out."

"Thanks, Elsie." The line clicked.

"Who was that?" Calamity plodded at Nona's heels when she came into the kitchen.

"Jenna Fairbanks, one of the volunteers with Found Hounds."

"Oh, yeah. That's the rescue group you got this dog from."

"Right." My rescue remorse was growing worse by the day.

"Got any coffee brewed, Mom?"

"Not yet. I'll start some. Did you sleep well last night with your furry friend?"

"Snug as a bug in a rug."

"Don't you mean like a basset in a blanket?"

Nona laughed. "She would have whined at the bedroom door all night if I hadn't let her in. It was the only way to shut her up."

"I know. Cruiser and I thank you, even if my new duvet is ruined."

"Sorry. I invited her onto my robe at the foot of the bed, but she obviously had other ideas."

"That's okay. I don't have anything around this house that isn't washable because drool rules here. I'm just glad we all finally got some sleep."

"Once she curled up next to me, she settled right down."

"It was probably the beat of your heart that calmed her."

"I never thought of that. That must be why they always say to put a ticking clock and a hot water bottle in with a new puppy. The pup thinks it's his mother."

"It's even better if they wrap the heated bottle in an old piece of fur. They settle right down. If she's like most rescues, she is probably a product of a puppy mill. They are taken from their mothers and litter mates at far too young an age, and all kinds of health and socialization problems result from it."

"Poor things. Gosh, you don't think she thinks I'm her mother, do you?"

"Could be. You're not very furry, though." Nona giggled and stroked Calamity. "She appears to be bonding with you much more than she has with me thus far. And she didn't take to Skip at all. Doesn't seem to like men, from what I've noticed."

"Smart dog." Nona's experiences with men hadn't been much better than Calamity's had. Perhaps they had more in common than she thought. The dog rested her chin on Nona's knee. "She sure is a needy little girl, isn't she? I guess her whole life has been a calamity up until now."

"Unfortunately." At the mention of her name, Calamity tried to jump in Nona's lap.

"Tell her 'off.' Good a time as any to start teaching her some manners."

"Why don't I just say 'down,' instead?"

"Because when you teach her to lie down, you'll use that command. She would get confused if you used the same command for both behaviors."

Nona said the word in her soft, sweet voice. "This one isn't working, either." They looked like they were in a boxing match as she tried to push the dog away. Calamity kept coming at her, sparring to gain the upper paw. I grabbed a couple of treat tidbits and placed them in Nona's hand.

"Now, repeat the command again, but this time say it louder and stronger. Be like an eagle, not a sparrow. The moment she obeys, give her a treat and praise her like crazy."

It took a few more tries, but finally stubborn Calamity obeyed Nona's command and stayed put. "It worked!"

"Well done. Maybe I can persuade you to take her to obedience school for me while you're here."

"Ha, ha. Very funny, Mother."

"Why not? She obviously likes you, and she'll need to pass obedience training before she can be placed in a permanent home."

"I'm no dog trainer. I've never even had a dog before. You know that."

I blamed myself for neglecting to introduce my daughter to a puppy when she was little. Dogs teach a child so many valuable lessons a parent can't. "You never know, you might meet some handsome young dog at the class." I could almost see the manhunt gears engage in Nona's brain. That suddenly put an entirely different spin on things.

"I'll think about it. By the way, I overheard some of your conversation on the phone earlier. Is there more trouble over at the shelter?"

"I'm afraid so."

"It's not another . . ."

"No, no. Not that. Someone broke into the shelter last night and released all the dogs."

"Released?"

"Or stole them."

"Who'd steal a bunch of stray mutts?"

"Hard to say. Possibly someone looking to turn a profit."

"Huh? How?"

"Not all dogs in shelters are mutts, as most people think. There are plenty of purebreds that could be sold to pet stores or research labs. Purebreds get stolen all the time from owners, too. Especially toy breeds, which are always popular."

"Maybe it could be some weird religious cult or something. There are so many creeps nowadays who might do harm to animals."

"Possibly. More likely it's the animal liberation group that's been picketing at the shelter."

"If that's true, then why did they only take the dogs? Why not the cats, too?"

Nona had a valid point. If TAILS was the group responsible for this, they would have freed the cats *and* the dogs, and probably the rabbits and hamsters, too. Heaven knew what Cruiser and I might find running loose in the forest on our next walk.

"Here's your coffee, Nona. Keep a close eye on Calamity for me, okay? Make sure she doesn't get into any trouble while Cruiser and I are gone."

"Will do. Where are you going?"

"To see who let the dogs out."

Chapter 12

In tailing the troublemaker who had unleashed havoc on Lakeside Animal Shelter, there was no better place to start than with Victoria Thatcher, the activist I'd met in the shelter parking lot. Something about her manner had sparked in me an instant aversion, and it wasn't just the purple hair or body piercings I'd found off-putting. At least I'd like to think it wasn't the obvious generation gap between us that was tainting my perception. Thank goodness Nona had never gone through a Goth phase like some youths do. She is much too beautiful to drape in black. When I'm an old woman, I may wear purple, but I vow that it won't be my hair color.

From what Tori had said to me that day, I deduced that she would have no qualms about rattling a few cages, or even cracking them open, in order to drive home her radical agenda for change at the shelter. Whether or not her tactics included murdering Rhoda Marx, no one had intimated as yet, but in my mind the possibility certainly existed.

TAILS headquarters wasn't easily found by letting your fingers walk through the Yellow Pages. The whole place had a subversive air to it, right down to its location, which was hidden behind a little-frequented mini-mall at the "Y" where Lake Tahoe Boulevard meets Highway 50. An outline of the word "NAILS" could still be discerned in the weathered wood beam above the door where lettering for the previous tenant, a nail salon, had been removed. I had to wonder why they hadn't substituted a "T" for the "N" and just kept the sign, but they clearly didn't want their whereabouts known to the general public. They might find people picketing on their own doorstep, especially when word got out about what had happened at the shelter.

Left to their own devices for very long, those released strays would form packs that might resort to preying upon livestock or pets for food, much like the coyotes that roam the forest behind my cabin. A pack of feral dogs could even attack a child! That wouldn't be good PR for TAILS if it turned out they were responsible for the break-in.

When I entered the anteroom with Cruiser in tow, I spotted a woman at a desk answering phones and asked her to direct me to the top dog. She spotted Cruiser and offered him a biscuit, which he eagerly snarfed, sliming the receptionist's hand before I could persuade him we weren't here to raid the cookie jar. She had to wipe the drool from her hand with a tissue before answering the next phone call. Occupational hazard. Like a four-legged snail, Cruiser left a glistening trail of slobber behind him as he meandered down the hall at his leisure, searching for more biscuits and sniffing where other dogs had left their mark, itching to leave his own pee-mail message. I'd taught him better, though. All piddling was to be done outdoors.

I found Tori Thatcher holed up in a cramped, paper-strewn office at the rear of the shop working at her computer. A large, tortoiseshell cat was curled beside the keyboard, trying to distract the typist with an occasional tail twitch. I hated to admit that, except for the cat, this space looked like my own office, wall-to-wall chaos. I couldn't quite make out what was on the computer screen, but when Tori saw me, she clicked on another window to hide whatever information wave she was surfing.

"Hi, Tori."

"Elsie MacBean. What brings you here?" She eyed me with her usual intensity. I didn't know if she was scowling because she had been concentrating and was annoyed at being interrupted, or if she was disappointed that I'd so easily ferreted out her secret lair. Perhaps both.

"I'd like to ask you a couple of questions. Got a moment?"

"I'm pretty busy right now, as you can see."

"I won't take up much of your time."

About then, Cruiser moseyed into the office. Tori's brow smoothed like an ironed sheet when she spotted him. She coaxed him to come to her, which he did. I was glad I'd brought my doggy diplomat along to break the ice.

"Hmm . . . okay. I guess I could use a break anyway. I've been at this for hours. Working at the computer too long makes my neck ache."

"I know the feeling. What are you writing?"

"An article for our next newsletter, *TAILS from the Front.*"

"Is this it?" I said, pointing to one of the piles on her desk. The cat took this as a cue to abandon her post beside the computer and drape herself across the desktop, right on the newsletter pile.

"Yup. Go ahead and take one."

"Thanks." I slipped a copy from under the office kitty and flipped through the eight-page glossy leaflet. It contained some graphic color photos of animals rescued from deplorable conditions. You'd have thought the shots were taken in a third-world country. They weren't. I set it back down on the splintered, coffee-ringed desk. "Nice quality newsletter you've got here." I didn't comment on the content. "Must cost a lot to produce."

"We believe the organization's funds are better spent on educating the public about animal welfare than on fancy office furniture." Looking around her office at the cat claw–shredded chairs and thrift store tables, I had to agree there was nothing fancy about the decor.

"I guess you must have heard about what happened over at Lakeside."

"Oh, you must be referring to the shelter manager's death."

"It's being called a homicide. I assumed you already knew about it."

"Why would you assume that?" Her brows knitted again. Someone needed to acquaint the hirsute Tori with the miracle of electrolysis for that unibrow of hers. Fortunately, she hadn't dyed her eyebrows purple, too. They'd have looked like an exotic caterpillar inching across the white page of her broad forehead. A lip wax wouldn't hurt either, but I was no one to talk. Growing a goatee is one side effect of being a middle-age woman that I hadn't anticipated.

"You read the newspaper, don't you?"

"I read them online. As you can see, I already have enough paper to wade through."

"Indeed you do."

"So, are you going to tell me what happened at the shelter or not?" Tori drummed her fingers on the desk. I knew I was in imminent danger of overstaying my welcome. Either that, or I'd struck a nerve. Perhaps there was really no need to tell her what I was about to.

"There was a break-in at the shelter last night."

"What do you mean?" She stopped drumming her fingers when the cat began batting at them. "A theft?"

"You could say that."

"What was stolen? Money?"

"Dogs."

Her caterpillar brow arched in surprise. Whether feigned or not, I couldn't tell. "Oh,

I see. And you obviously think we had something to do with this."

"Isn't that what your group is about? Animal liberation?"

"Of course we are, but we wouldn't just release animals from a facility without assuring they'd be properly cared for. That would be irresponsible and harmful to the animals and to the community."

"So you're saying you would liberate them if you *did* have the means to care for them?"

For the first time since I'd met her, the cat had Tori's tongue.

Chapter 13

My chat with the TAILS ringleader hadn't been nearly as productive as I'd hoped. I'm usually a good people reader, but Tori Thatcher would be a perfect Stateline card dealer with that poker face of hers. For all I knew, she moonlighted at Caesar's when she wasn't breaking and entering animal facilities.

TAILS headquarters seemed to be the logical place to begin my search for the person responsible for unleashing havoc on the shelter and the community at large. What better suspect than a fanatical animal liberation group, more specifically their lead dog? In my mind, it wasn't much of a leap from some of their malicious acts committed at animal facilities to murdering a reviled shelter manager.

At any rate, my ensuing investigation provided Cruiser with a nice, long car ride. There's nothing he enjoys more than hanging his head out the car window, ears flapping in the breeze. As we drove west on Lake Tahoe Boulevard, I scanned the roadside for any sign of stray dogs, as Jenna had asked me to do. All I spotted were dogs being led on leashes. At least I felt assured that those dogs would never end up in a shelter or under the wheels of a car on a busy South Tahoe thoroughfare. Then I thought of the millions of dogs who aren't so lucky, but I had to put them out of mind, at least for the moment. I had only begun to sniff around on this case, and who better to help me do it than Cruiser? As if in response, I heard the familiar snuffle of my sleuth's nose sampling the air for scents as we approached the shelter.

Lakeside Shelter looked quiet — too quiet for a workday. I saw only one or two cars in the lot I didn't recognize as belonging to the staff. No cars meant no adoptions, but that's because there were few animals left at the shelter to adopt, at least until more strays were rounded up, as they surely would be. A couple of people had come to adopt kittens. There is always a surplus of kitties in the summertime.

I also noticed that there were no demonstrators congregated outside the entrance of the shelter today. Perhaps they were lying low for a while, either because they were responsible for the break-in at the shelter or were afraid that people would assume they were responsible for it, and worse. A murder rap wouldn't do their cause much good . . . or would it? There was something about Tori Thatcher that made me believe there was nothing she wouldn't do to focus public attention on their cause. Even if her group could prove they had no involvement in the Marx murder, spotlighting the mismanagement of a shelter and animal overpopulation issues would be furthered in the bargain.

When Cruiser and I entered the shelter, we were met by Amanda Peabody.

"Hey, Cruiser, how are you, boy? Want a treat?" *Ask a silly question.* Funny how dog lovers always greet the hounds before the humans. Amanda reached into the biscuit jar on the counter and offered Cruiser a tidbit. He snatched it up and then begged for another.

"At this rate, I'll never have to feed him again. He can beg for treats everywhere we go. He just scored some at the TAILS office."

"I heard you went there. Did you get to talk to Victoria Thatcher?"

"Yes, but how did you know I was going there?"

"I overheard Jenna talking to you on the phone."

"Is she still here?"

"No." Amanda offered Cruiser another treat and proceeded to quiz me. "What did Tori have to say?"

"Not much."

"Maybe the tongue ring got in her way."

"Something had hold of her tongue, that's for sure. She's one cool cookie."

"She's just a San Francisco snob who thinks she can come to our community and stir up trouble."

"Hey, back up the cable car, Amanda. I'm from San Francisco, too."

"You are? Sorry, I didn't know that."

"That's okay. You couldn't have known. I don't like to make rash judgments about people, not even Tori Thatcher. Maybe she's not so different from you and me."

"How so?"

"She also does what she can for the welfare of animals, only she does it in a more confrontational manner."

"Murdering a shelter manager is pretty confrontational, all right." Amanda slipped Cruiser another treat.

"What makes you so certain she's behind

Rhoda Marx's murder?"

"Who else would it be? You know TAILS has been causing trouble here because of her. I even overheard Tori threaten Rhoda one day."

"You did? What did she say to her?"

"I don't recall her exact words, but it was something like, 'It's you who should be gassed, not the animals.' "

"Wow! What did Rhoda say?"

"She said nothing, but that's how she always responded to people who were angry with her. Her silence only served to make them angrier. It wasn't the first time someone threatened her."

"Really? Who else has made threats against her?"

"A better question would be, who hasn't?"

"She was really that terrible to work for?"

"Yes, she was. I knew one day somebody was going to get even with her somehow, but I always thought it would be one of her co-workers, not an outsider."

"How do you know it wasn't a co-worker?"

"I don't know, but I'd like to think I haven't been working side by side with a murderer all this time."

Rex suddenly came to mind. If anyone looked like trouble, it was he.

"Who is the newest employee at the shelter?"

"I'm not sure. There's a high staff turnaround here."

"You must keep employee records."

"Sure."

"If it's on a computer file, can you e-mail it to me? I'd also like to know who's been here the longest and who was the last person to leave your employ. I'd like a list of volunteers, too."

"I don't know if it's filed on the computer. We're a little behind in technology here. Anyway, I'm not authorized to release that information to the public, Elsie."

"I'm sure you can give it to Sheriff Cassidy, then. This is a murder investigation."

"I still can't believe something like this happened here at our little Tahoe shelter."

"Tahoe isn't immune to crime, not even murder. No place is."

"I probably shouldn't say this, but things have been much better here since Rhoda's been gone. There'll be a replacement soon, though."

"Why don't you apply for the opening, Amanda?"

"I doubt if I'd ever be considered for the position. The City Council will probably make another appointment."

"Is that how Rhoda got her job?"

"Yes. It's always who you know. I don't think she'd have been appointed on her merits alone. I only hope the next manager will be an improvement on her."

"From what you've told me, sounds like whoever it is couldn't be much worse."

"I hope not."

"Well, Cruiser and I had better get going . . . Cruiser, where are you?" As usual, he had done his disappearing act while I was distracted. It wouldn't be hard to find him, though. All I had to do was follow the drips of slobber on the concrete, like a track of breadcrumbs in the forest. There were so many different scents in the shelter for him to explore, it was no wonder he'd wandered off. Amanda trailed me as I followed the drool down one corridor then the next until I came upon Cruiser frozen in front of an empty kennel marked 9. The kennel door was the only one on the corridor opened wide. Cruiser stood in front of K-9, holding to a point like a dog that is trained to hunt more than biscuits and Beggin' Strips. His hind legs were a-quiver with excitement or fear, or both. I'd seen him do that before, always when danger lurked nearby. Then, he lifted his nose to the ceiling and let out the most sorrowful howl.

CHAPTER 14

The trail of red paw prints began in one corner of Kennel 9, led out the kennel door and down the corridor. Amanda and I both stood staring at the bloody prints. We were frozen in place like Cruiser, who seemed to sense something we couldn't. Amanda's face was whiter than Cruiser's belly in a snowdrift.

"You look as though you've seen a ghost," I said.

"I'm not sure I haven't."

"What do you mean?"

"Every time anyone comes down this corridor, the kennel door is thrown wide open like it is now."

"What's so unusual about that?"

"It's always locked."

I looked at the latch. There was a lock hanging on the door, but it was unlatched. It hadn't been jimmied.

"It's not locked now. Who has the keys?"

"We keep them on a big O-ring. Rex carries it around with him most of the time. But no dogs are kenneled in this cage. We haven't used it since that terrible incident with Gilda."

"I remember it well. Poor Gilda." I could still see the headlines of the article I had written in the *Tattler*. Gilda, also a basset hound, was the unfortunate victim of Lakeside policy that had been the catalyst for all the troubles going on at the shelter in the past few weeks. After her sad, wrinkly countenance appeared in every newspaper in the Tahoe basin and beyond, she had become the poster pup for raising public awareness about poorly run shelters. Gilda was one of many dogs that never came home.

"We've had problems with other dogs who were kept in the kennel, so we've become a little superstitious about it," Amanda said.

"What kinds of problems?"

"We've had several dogs go kennel crazy after spending only a few hours inside. That usually happens over a longer time. One bitch killed her pups after we put her in there. And now this."

"So, what are you saying? This kennel is haunted?"

"I don't believe in ghosts, but I do believe

in curses. I think it's cursed because a bad thing happened here."

"I'll buy that." I am no stranger to the world of the unseen. This wasn't my first experience with strange occurrences in and around Lake Tahoe. With me, it's as hereditary as Cruiser's long ears and keen nose. Like him, I can sense things that aren't immediately evident. Some signs come to me in dreams and visions. The Washoe believe in all manner of things most people don't, like water spirits of the lake and ancient, fearsome creatures. Tahoe is not without its share of ghosts and curses. However, this was my first encounter with a cursed kennel at the local animal shelter, bloody paw prints and all.

Cruiser was behaving very strangely, even for a nosy basset hound. His noggin' was bobbling the same way it does out in the woods when he's caught the scent of a squirrel or some other creature with that super-sniffer nose of his. As in the field, I had no choice but to follow his lead.

He waddled down the corridor of the shelter in the direction of the ominous crimson paw prints. What could it mean? I had seen many strange phenomena in my lifetime that couldn't be easily explained away, but I had never seen bloody prints appear out of nowhere. They were usually accompanied by a corpse, which made me wonder what horror we might discover at the end of this bloody trail.

Amanda and I followed close behind Cruiser as though we were at the end of an invisible leash. He led us straight through the kennel, past the string of empty cages. We trailed him down the gray mile all the way to the euthanasia chamber, where the paw prints abruptly ended. The prints at the end of the trail looked fresher and wetter than the ones near K-9.

"This is really strange," Amanda said.

I bent down and dipped my forefinger in one of the prints. "Something strange is going on here, all right," I said. "Your bleeding ghost has two legs instead of four, Amanda."

"What do you mean?"

"This isn't blood, it's red paint."

Chapter 15

The fake bloodstains at the shelter had me befuddled. Who put them there, and why were the prints leading from Kennel 9 to the place where the lifeless body of Rhoda Marx had been discovered only days before? What was the connection? Could it be a warning of more trouble to come? The threat of another murder about to be committed? Who would be the next victim?

Clearly, it was some kind of spoof or scare tactic from someone who had an ax to grind with the shelter. I assumed it was the handiwork of one of the TAILS activists, who might have opened all of the cages for the animals to escape into the adjoining woods. If that had been the idea behind the break-in, it certainly wouldn't benefit the animals.

It could also be a disgruntled employee or volunteer who worked in the shelter or had worked there at some time in the past. It was clear that someone was intent on causing more trouble at Lakeside Shelter. Perhaps that's what Cruiser really sensed. Trouble. The question was, from whom, or what, would it come?

Of course, with Cruiser it could have been the lingering bouquet of some hot little bitch that had set him to sniffing around the shelter, not that my neutered male would know what to do with one if he found her. Speaking of little bitches, I began to wonder what trouble that naughty Calamity was getting into behind Nona's back in my absence. I decided it was time to go find out.

Cruiser and I made tracks for the MacBean cabin, but we weren't the only ones. As I drove past the sheriff's office, Skip's patrol car veered out right in front of me. I laid on the horn, and he scowled at me in his rearview mirror. I knew he was wondering who would be brave enough or stupid enough to honk at The Law to get out of the way. When he spotted me with my copilot, the fuzzy orange caterpillar mustache on his upper lip handle-barred in a big grin. He pulled over and waved for me to come up alongside.

"Hey, Beanie. What a coincidence. I was just heading over to your place."

Now, that was a big surprise. It was almost high noon, and this lawman always seemed to end up at my place right around mealtimes in the hope I was cooking up some veggie chili. He was in luck today. I'd cooked and frozen a big batch of it because I knew Nona was coming up. She loves my chili too, like her dad did. All that was required was a little defrosting in the trusty microwave.

"Why, what's up?"

"I have some new information on the Marx case. Feed me lunch, and I'll tell you about it."

"All right, Skip. Follow the bouncing basset."

"Lead on."

I drove ahead and Skip pulled in behind me, giving a playful retaliatory blast on his siren. Cruiser bayed in response. Now I was the one shooting daggers at Skip in my rearview mirror. "Smart alec sheriff," I muttered. "Just for that I'm putting an extra shot of Tabasco in your chili."

Driving back to my place, I began to wonder what Skip was going to tell me about the Marx case. What new piece of evidence had turned up? Had he already made an arrest? And if he had, was it the right person? After all, he's the law in these parts. I'm just a reporter who moonlights as a private investigator, although these days it seems more like the other way around. But Skip isn't always as intuitive as he might be. He tends to rely more on hard evidence than gut feelings, and that's his job. Evidence is important and can't be ignored, but you can also get a sense about things and people that is often every bit as conclusive — a psychic fingerprint. In that way, I'm a lot like Cruiser. He uses all his senses.

When I drove up to my cabin, I had a pretty strong sense about what I might find when I entered the front door. All Nona would have to do was get distracted for a little while, and Calamity would get into trouble. But when Cruiser and I entered the house, everything appeared to be in order. No upturned wastebaskets or shredded paper were strewn about the house. Nona was reading a book, and Calamity was lying at her feet, sleeping peacefully. Of course, the moment she saw us come in, that was the end of the serene scene. She raced over to greet Cruiser and me.

When she tried to jump up on me, I pushed her back down. I told her to sit and then rewarded her with a tidbit before giving her the attention she craved. She didn't jump up again. Slowly, I felt like I was making some progress with my new foster.

Basset hounds are much brainier than they get credit for. Beneath that nonchalant, innocent exterior is a cool, calculating intelligence. Like a mystery novelist and the criminals they write about, bassets are forever plotting and scheming their next caper while their owners are usually clueless. Calamity was no exception. I had no doubt there were plenty of behavior hurdles left for us to surmount before she could be considered adoptable.

"You were gone quite a while," Nona said.

"I had a few things to attend to. Did you have any trouble with Calamity?"

"Not at all. She's been as quiet as a mouse the whole time you were gone."

"That's what worries me."

"What's for lunch, Mom? I'm starved."

"How's chili sound?"

"Yummy!"

"Good, Skip's joining us. He should be pulling up pretty soon. I don't know where he is. He was right behind me."

"Maybe he got a call or something."

"Could be. I'll go ahead and warm it up."

"Good. If he doesn't show, that means there'll be more for us."

Chapter 16

Skip drove up half an hour later.

"What happened to you? I thought you were right behind us."

"I stopped to grab a cold brewskie to wash down that famous five-alarm chili of yours."

"Your beans await you, Sheriff. Have some fresh garlic bread, too." Skip sat down at the kitchen table to delve into his bowl of red.

"Please, don't say beans," he said.

"Why not?"

"Because it reminds me of the bean counters who are cutting back our funding for the next fiscal year. We were long overdue for a raise and some new crime lab equipment, but now that's all down the tubes."

"The economy is bad everywhere, Skip. They're having the same troubles at the shelter."

"I may even have to lay off some staff.

That means more work for you-know-who."

"I thought you seemed a little stressed out lately. What about your new rookie, Rusty? She'll be some help to you, won't she?"

"I don't know. She's still pretty wet behind the ears."

"Looked like she was handling things pretty well on the Marx case."

"It's just that there are guys who have been with the department longer who might resent her advancing too quickly in the ranks."

Seems like I'd bumped my head against this glass ceiling myself plenty of times in the past on the job. "Why? Because she's a woman? And pretty, too?"

"There're laws against discrimination on the job, Beanie. You know that."

"Yeah, but it still happens anyway. And you know that!"

"I have to admit the fact that she was a *Playboy* centerfold doesn't help matters."

"She was? How do you know that?"

"I caught one of the guys with her pin-up in his locker."

"Did you make him take it down?"

"Of course."

"You didn't put it up in your own locker, did you?" Skip has always been a pushover for a pretty face or a shapely figure, as he'd proved many times before. Rusty Cannon had both.

"Don't be ridiculous. I threw it in the trash."

"What difference does it make what this woman did before she joined your department or does after hours on her own time?" Nona interjected. "There are lots of women and even some men who have modeled for men's magazines to get through college or whatever their goal might be."

Nona had that right. I only hoped none of her Victoria's Secret work was taped inside a locker at some police station.

"It doesn't make a bit of difference to me, but it might to some," Skip said, shifting in his seat. I noticed a rolled-up piece of paper poking out of Skip's hip pocket. About that time Calamity wandered into the kitchen, investigating the source of the aroma of food. She edged up to Skip and snatched at the corner of the paper in his pocket. Out it came. Skip slapped at his pocket but he was too slow on the draw this time. "Hey, bring that back here!"

"Calamity! Drop it!" I commanded. She didn't, of course, but began shaking the paper like a terrier with a rat. I managed to grab it away and began to smooth it out as best I could. Then I saw what it was. I unfolded a foldout of the voluptuous redhead, Miss March, none other than "Busty Rusty" Cannon. "Threw it in the trash, huh?"

Skip snatched the paper away. When his face flushed, it wasn't because of my spicy chili but something a lot spicier. "I forgot it was in there. I really did intend to throw it away."

"No time like the present." I wasn't sure, but I thought I saw a tear roll down Skip's cheek as he tore up the tattered centerfold and threw it in the trash container.

"What's wrong, Skip?" His complexion was nearly the color of the chili. Sweat beaded on his temples.

"What did you put in this stuff? Lava?" Skip mopped his brow with a corner of my tablecloth.

"It's a lot spicier than your usual, Mom." Even Nona was breaking a sweat, and she never does. "Trying out a new recipe on us?"

"I added some jalapeno peppers and a couple of other secret ingredients to the mix. Too hot?"

"Was the Angora firestorm too hot?" Skip said, chugging down his beer.

"Be glad I left out the extra Tabasco sauce in yours. I was going to get even with you for blasting Cruiser and me with your siren."

"Don't worry, you did." I wasn't sure if he was referring to my chili or the shredded centerfold.

Nona was doing okay, but then she had been reared on the red stuff at the Mac-Bean house. "You really ought to think about competing in one of those chili cook-offs, Mom. This is the best batch you've ever made."

"Yeah, and now it's the hottest, too," Skip said as he polished off the last of his bowlful.

"Maybe someday when I get tired of selling my words and snooping around crime scenes, I'll sell chili. Anyway, I'd rather make it for my friends and family."

"Yeah, 'cause we're your guinea pigs." Skip leaned back in his chair and heaved a contented sigh. "Whew, I'm stuffed!"

"Well-fed guinea pigs, though." I playfully patted Skip's rounded belly.

"Gee, thanks." I could tell Skip didn't appreciate my comment. He'd never let on, but I know he is sensitive about his thickening waist and thinning hair, especially around pretty young gals like Nona and Rusty.

I didn't like hurting Skip's feelings so I changed the subject. "You said if I fed you

you'd tell me what you have on the Marx case."

"That's right. I did, didn't I?"

"What did you find out from the M.E.?"

"Well, the autopsy showed . . ."

"Hey, if you guys are gonna talk crime and cadavers, I'm outta here," Nona said. "Come on, Calamity, let's go keep Cruiser company." Calamity's toenails clicked like castanets on the kitchen floor as she trotted along behind Nona.

"Looks like Nona has a new friend."

"It's funny how dogs choose their people. This little dog bonded with Nona from the first moment, like Cruiser bonded with Tom. It was only after Tom died that Cruiser and I became close. Until then, he was Tom's dog."

"Yeah, I remember how much Tom loved Cruiser."

"It was mutual."

"And now it's the same for you and Cruiser."

"I think dogs know what we need better than we know ourselves. Maybe that's why Calamity has chosen my daughter. Nona needs a good friend. She's kind of like her mother, a bit of a loner."

"She lives in a big city. How can you be alone in a big city? That is, unless you breathe on someone after eating a whole loaf of garlic bread." Skip popped a Tic Tac in his mouth.

"It can be a lot lonelier in a big city than in a small town. In a small town, everyone knows who you are, and people are more inclined to reach out to one another. You can get lost in a metropolis like San Francisco. I should know."

"That's right. I forgot you grew up there. As it so happens, so did Rhoda Marx."

"Maybe that's part of the reason no one around here liked her much. She was an outsider."

"Could be." When Skip scratched his mustache, it looked like he was tickling a caterpillar.

"Someone disliked her enough to kill her. That's got to be about more than being an outsider."

"Wrong, Beanie. More than one person hated Rhoda Marx enough to murder her."

"What do you mean?"

"Because she was already dead before somebody put her in that chamber and turned on the gas."

Chapter 17

What Skip told me over chili and garlic bread had me stumped. He explained that a blow to Rhoda's skull had killed her, not the gas in the euthanasia chamber. That's why the tissue inside her mouth wasn't the color of cherries (or my chili), as it would be if she had died from CO poisoning. But if she was already dead, why put her in the gas tank? Had her murder been a team effort? She clearly had made plenty of enemies in the community, including some on her own staff. And of course there was TAILS, always lurking about, raising my suspicion about these activists' motives. Had she been killed elsewhere and her body placed in the chamber to make a point about animal cruelty? None of it made any sense. Not to me or to Skip, either. Meanwhile, Marx's murderer was still on the loose, and the trail was going colder by the day. And perhaps there was more than one stray suspect unleashed on the community.

Besides the death of Rhoda Marx, other matters closer to home were weighing on my mind. I was worried about Nona. After what my daughter had told me about discovering a suspicious lump, I understood why she had decided to take a hiatus from work, particularly at a time when her career was going so well. Nona is too much like her mother sometimes. She's as driven to succeed in modeling as I am to succeed at writing.

Some traits skip generations, and Nona's head-in-the-sand reluctance to find out for certain whether the lump was really anything to worry about was very much like her grandmother's had been. Unfortunately, my mother should not have ignored her symptoms as long as she did. In retrospect, I should have noticed her crushing fatigue when we walked in the forest together, instead of discounting it to advancing age. Perhaps we were both in denial about her failing health. You don't like to think about the possibility of losing someone you love. I vowed not to make the same mistake with Nona.

I certainly could understand her trepidation and why she was distrustful of the standard invasive medical treatments, should she have a malignant tumor. I'd seen my mother go through that agony to no avail. While her life may have been prolonged, her quality of life was dubious.

No one has yet discovered for certain what causes cancer. Whether it's a virus, faulty genes, poor lifestyle choices, environmental pollution, or a combination of all these, I have no doubt that stress is also an often-overlooked factor in human diseases. The negative effect of prolonged stress upon any living organism is undeniable, and Nona's life has certainly been stressful the past few years. I'm not just referring to the demands of making her mark in the world of supermodels, constantly striving to achieve physical perfection by whatever means. At least Nona hasn't had any part of her body surgically altered for the camera. She's so naturally gorgeous it isn't necessary, but she has struggled constantly with her weight, like her mother and even her mother's dog. I also can't discount the fact that she's been unlucky in love, nor can I ignore the effect that her near-death experience at the hands of the murderous Medwyn that terrible winter of the Tahoe Terror might have had on her. I couldn't help blaming myself in some measure for Nona's problems. She would never have been in harm's way if it weren't for her meddlesome mother who is always getting involved in crime.

In my experience with rescuing dogs for Found Hounds and having seen what long-term stress can do to dogs, including cancer and other health and behavior problems, I understand that we have more in common with our canine brethren than we might imagine, as research scientists are discovering in their studies of human diseases like cancer. I had always believed it wasn't an accident that Cruiser appeared when he did, just before the most devastating time in my life — Tom's death. Perhaps it was also no accident that Calamity had come along at a time when Nona was facing her greatest life challenge. I am certain that Calamity sensed Nona needed a friend, and there's no doubt that Calamity needed one, too.

My greatest challenge at the moment was the prospect of having to deal with Ms. Littlefeather, tribal elder and media darling. Wherever there was a TV camera, you'd find her right in front of it. She's no shrinking violet, that's for sure, and it's good that someone like her speaks for our people's interests in the community. That aside, I knew that having to ask her for advice was going to stick in my craw like a pinecone, but I'd do anything for my daughter, even make nice to my old rival.

I caught up with Sonseah that afternoon as she was leaving the local TV station, where she had just talked with newscasters about the Washoe tribe's growing contention over a large tract of native land on the West Shore being threatened by development. If there was one thing Lake Tahoe didn't need more of to sully its cobalt blue waters, it was more land development. The struggle to preserve tribal land in the Tahoe Basin is ongoing, and I felt bad that I hadn't been right there with Sonseah on TV to help her defend our heritage, but I had too many irons in the fire already, and they were heating up fast.

"Elsie MacBean, what brings *you* here?"

She said it like I'd never had any previous experience with the media. Didn't she know what I do for a living? Her arrogance apparently knew no bounds. At least she wasn't festooned in her usual ceremonial regalia, which made her appear haughtier. For Nona's sake, I swallowed my pride.

"I need to talk to you. Can you spare a moment?"

"I have some time before my next personal appearance. There's a little coffee shop around the corner. We can talk there."

I followed Sonseah to a cozy little coffee shop. Perk Up was a retro java joint, with no fancy coffee drinks or screeching cappuccino machines. Sonseah had always seemed to me more like the Starbuck's type. She looked like someone with exotic tastes in everything, including her caffeine, but to my surprise she ordered straight black coffee. Gosh, did anyone really serve that anymore in cafés? Only at places where waitresses with red beehives, like Rita Ramirez, pour the coffee. I treated Sonseah to her coffee, since she was taking time to schedule me between TV spots.

"Now, what did you want to talk to me about?"

"It's about my daughter, Nona."

"Such a beautiful girl."

"Thank you. Yes, she is beautiful." The way Sonseah said it, she almost sounded as though Nona and I couldn't possibly be related. She had never seen photos of me when I was Nona's age. We could be twins, even if Nona was a bit taller and slenderer. She got that from her father.

"There's nothing wrong with her, is there?"

Was Sonseah a mind reader? No, she was probably just reading my body language, much like Cruiser does. I'm sure that my concern about Nona was practically oozing from every pore. Could she scent pheromones of fear like a dog can?

"Yes, she's found a suspicious lump."

"Oh, I'm so sorry, Elsie." Sonseah's tone was suddenly entirely different than I had ever heard come from her until now. With her next words, I understood why.

"My mother had breast cancer."

"So did mine." I didn't mention that she hadn't survived it. I didn't want to speak the words aloud for fear it might jinx Nona. I also didn't want to entertain thoughts of another disastrous prognosis.

"Believe me, I understand what you're going through. Is there anything I can do to help?"

Unlike when I'd heard some people mouth such well-meaning platitudes, I believed that she really meant it.

"Yes, there is, Sonseah."

"Why don't you call me Sonny? Everyone does."

Everyone but me until now. "Sure. Sonny it is." I didn't even know this woman had a nickname or would even want to be referred to by anything other than her formal name. Perhaps that was just her public persona. I was seeing a new side to my old nemesis I hadn't ever known existed. Sometimes people wear masks, letting you see only what they want you to see. Not everyone is an open book like I am.

"You may as well call me Beanie, too."

A warm, empathetic smile softened her angular features. It was a different smile from any I'd seen on Sonseah's face — when she smiled at all. "Just tell me what you need, Beanie."

"Nona wants to have a healing ceremony with the tribe. Do you think you could arrange it for us?"

"Yes, I'd be glad to do that. When did you want to do it?"

"As soon as possible."

"Okay. I'll give you a call when it's all set up. Keep it under your hat, though."

"Of course. Thanks so much, Sons—"

"It's Sonny, remember?"

"Sonny." Boy, I must be in Sonseah's inner circle now. Sarcasm aside, it felt good to talk with someone of my own tribe who really understood what we were possibly facing. Having a family history of the disease made the odds of Nona having a malignancy much greater. Like Scarlett O'Hara, I wouldn't think about that now. I'd think about that tomorrow.

CHAPTER 18

Cruiser can be pretty demanding about his walks. I try to limit him to two a day, but he sometimes has other ideas. Often I feel like I should be earning my living as a professional dog walker. He's not a young dog, so I don't like to overdo a good thing, especially at nearly 7,000 feet altitude. Like some other dog breeds with deep chest cavities, bassets can be candidates for bloat and gastric torsion, which can be fatal, so when I exercise him, I'm very careful not to feed or water him within two hours before or after.

However, Calamity was a young dog and full of energy that needed to be expended at regular intervals so she didn't get into mischief. Keeping her active might help prevent her from wreaking havoc in my house. I only hoped I had the energy to keep up with her. Having Nona with me would be a big help, especially since she and

Calamity appeared to have bonded like peanut butter and jelly from the get-go. You never know who a dog will form an attachment to, but they choose their human companions as surely as we choose them.

The setting sun filtered through the dense stand of pines behind the cabin, and a cooling breeze brushed the treetops. It was time for a last walk up the hill with Cruiser and Calamity before darkness fell.

"Ready for a walk, guys?" Silly question. All I had to do was make a move for the leashes, and Cruiser was up and in formation for his evening excursion. Dogs are experts at reading our body language, and Calamity was already an apt pupil of Cruiser's. She knew something good must be about to happen if Cruiser was getting so excited about it. Nona's getting up to join the outing was all that was needed to spark the new dog's interest in going for a walk.

The only trouble was that I knew she had no leash training. Calamity's paw pads were so pink and smooth I doubted if she had ever been outside a cage in her life. I guessed she was probably a puppy mill dog, which could certainly account for her lack of socialization and fearfulness of every new situation. Being in a poorly run pound hadn't helped improve her puppy mill issues any. A walk in the forest was no doubt going to present a whole new challenge for her, and for us. But inhaling some fresh mountain air before retiring for the night would help me sleep better.

This certainly wasn't the first time I'd walked more than one dog at a time in the woods, but it was the first time I'd ever walked one with no clue about the purpose of a leash. If this were a field trial, I could let my brace of two bassets range free to sniff at will, but if I did that with Calamity, she'd probably head straight for the hills. I made the mistake of using an extendable leash to walk her in the forest. This was like threading the leashes through an agility course as the dogs wound through the scrub brush and pine trees ahead of us, getting more tangled by the minute.

Of course, Cruiser has never been above playing bread and butter with trees, light posts, or anything else you can wrap a leash around. It's the nature of a stubborn, scent-driven basset to head in the opposite direction you have a mind to go. When you feel a firm tug on the line with a seventy-pound hound at the other end, it's usually you who gets reeled in, not the dog. At least I had Nona along with me to help untangle the leads as we went along. I could tell she was losing patience, though.

"This is impossible, Mom. I think Calamity needs some leash training before we attempt another walk."

"I think you're right." Of course, I wasn't doing much better with Cruiser, who wanted to sniff every tree and shrub in the forest. "It's getting late. We'd better head back to the cabin before it gets too dark."

The forest was enveloped in shadows as the sun made its final stand against the purpling peaks of Mount Tallac. The rising crescent moon looked like a dog's tail wagging on the eastern horizon. Just when we managed to point the dogs in the direction of home, I heard a thudding on the ground among the trees to my right. I glanced in time to see a pair of deer, a buck and a doe, dashing through the forest.

The buck's antlers clattered among the pine branches as the magnificent animal crashed through the thick woods. Velvet brown eyes were wide with fear as the deer fled a predator or some other imminent peril. Other than coyotes, they had few natural predators left at Tahoe. I had heard no coyote packs since we'd been out in the forest. That left only the hunter or a forest fire to account for the deer bolting through the trees. At least that's what I imagined until I heard the sounds of distinctly canine yips and barks that trailed the fleeing deer down the mountainside.

Both Cruiser and Calamity froze in their tracks. Cruiser lifted his muzzle to the cool night air, sniffed the subtle scents carried upon the wind currents, and bayed. His novitiate, Calamity, emitted a few tentative barks before her pendulous lips formed a perfect "O" and she joined Cruiser in a true basset chorus. By now, I understood every nuance of Cruiser's utterances and what they meant. I knew he wasn't begging for Bacon Strips. This was a warning!

"Mom! Look over there!" Nona pointed toward a stand of pines from which the deer had emerged moments before. Among the shadows of the pines on the forest floor, I could make out the silhouette of the pack of wild canines chasing after the deer. It was not a sight foreign to me. I had spent much more time hiking these mountains than my daughter had, so the appearance of coyotes was not cause for alarm. I had often seen packs of coyotes tracking their prey in the waning hours of day and heard their cries echoing from deep in the woods on moonlit nights. I had no fear of them. Attacks upon humans are rare. They are usually more afraid of us than we are of them, although I understood that the coyote's howl could make the hair on a tenderfoot's neck spike like a dog's ruff.

"It's a coyote pack chasing the deer. They won't bother us." The words had no sooner left my mouth than one of the animals stopped short in his pursuit and stepped from the shadows into a silver beam of moonlight. It was then I realized that this was no coyote pack tracking deer but a pack of feral dogs. We all stood frozen in place as the large, white German shepherd dog edged closer to us. Fur bristling, his lips curled over sharp fangs in a menacing growl. I recognized the animal from a previous less-threatening encounter. It was Spirit, the shepherd I had seen at Lakeside Shelter the day I adopted Calamity.

Now Spirit looked like a ghost dog with his coat glistening like fresh fallen snow in the moonbeams. I had been impressed with the sheer size of the animal when I first saw him at the shelter and thought he was beautiful, but my perspective was now very different out here in the forest surrounded by a pack of wild, hungry dogs.

Several of the other dogs abruptly ceased their pursuit of the deer and joined the shepherd at the forest's edge. We weren't running away like frightened deer, so I suppose we looked like easier prey to them than the buck and doe. We didn't have sharp antlers to attack them with, either. In fact, we had nothing to fight them off with, not even a walking stick, which I often carried when hiking. Nona and I were as frightened as the deer. The trick was not to let the feral dogs know it.

"Don't move a muscle, Nona. If we turn to run, they'll be after us in a flash. We don't stand a chance of outrunning them." I knew we stood even less chance of escaping the pack with the two slowpokes, Cruiser and Calamity, tagging along with us. They couldn't fend off an attack from the dogs. They'd be killed for sure.

Half a dozen other dogs of various breeds flanked the large, powerful shepherd. Most were mixed breeds, but I could make out a couple of purebreds in the group. All were medium-sized to large animals. Spirit, the largest among them, was clearly the alpha of the pack. Like a general commanding his troops, he growled his commands to them to stand their ground. None were backing down.

"They aren't rabid, are they, Mom?"

"No, I don't think so. Just a bunch of starving strays."

"What are we going to do?"

"If we can somehow scare off the big guy, the rest will probably follow suit."

"Good. How do we do that?"

"I'm thinking, Papoose. I'm thinking."

"Think faster!"

Chapter 19

The wind had picked up and was howling through the forest like a pack of hungry coyotes, but it wasn't a coyote pack that confronted us now. The feral dogs were becoming harder to discern among the shadowed pines in the enveloping night. Was that shape moving out there in the darkness an animal, tail erect and quivering, ready to pounce, or merely a sapling waving in the breeze? The imagination plays tricks on you when you're scared, and I confess that I was scared silly. So was Nona. I couldn't tell if the knocking sound I heard was her knees or mine, but we both heard the threatening guttural growls of the wild dogs and the crunch of pine needles beneath their paws as they closed in on two frightened women and a brace of bassets.

"Back away slowly, but don't make any sudden movements. Avoid any direct eye contact. They'll perceive that as a threat."

Nona followed my lead. We both stepped backward a couple of paces, but when we retreated, the pack advanced. We inched back a few more feet, slowly trying to reel in Cruiser and Calamity as we did. Calamity finally responded to the tugs on her leash, but Cruiser wouldn't budge. My foolishly stubborn dog was determined to stand his ground.

Calamity began to tremble and whine, but a deep rumble rose from Cruiser's throat that seemed to come from the tip of his tail and resonated in his barrel chest. He was alpha of his pack and prepared to defend it, come what may. His challenge was answered by the menacing snarl of Spirit and his cohorts. In the moonlight I could see the shepherd's muscles tensing up for an attack.

"Cruiser, hush." I knew if he continued his growling, the confrontation could quickly escalate and we'd be in big trouble. He'd given a good account of himself in the past against a lone canine adversary, aptly dubbed the Tahoe Terror, but he'd never manage to fend off an entire pack. Yet I knew he'd die trying to protect us in an ear-tearing fight, and I couldn't let that happen to my brave boy. What to do? What to do? There were no rocks around nearby to use as weapons. As a last resort, I picked up a large pinecone lying at my feet and hurled it at the shepherd, hoping to scare him away. It had no effect. Spirit didn't even flinch. He only growled louder as he began to draw closer, his posture stiffening for the assault.

"What are we going to do, Mom?"

I didn't answer, because I really didn't know what else to do.

"Mother?"

I thought of my own dear mother and how we often used to walk together in these woods from the time I was a child. I always felt so safe with her close beside me. I remembered how Mama taught me the secrets of nature and unlocked a magical spirit world for me, as her ancestors before her had done for their children. She knew every tree, rock, and rivulet of the Tahoe landscape like the deep creases in the palms of her own weathered hands.

As I visualized my beloved mother, I fancied I heard her calling my name in the wind that moaned through the forest. "El-si-nore." When I heard her strong, reassuring voice on the wind, I felt my fear melt away, and I instinctively knew we'd be all right. She would protect us . . . somehow.

Just then, a powerful wind gust ripped through the topmost branches of the pines towering above us. The trees waved and whipped wildly in the gale. I heard an explosive crack from somewhere close by, and I knew what that meant. I had heard those sounds echo through the woods before in a storm, but there was usually no one around to shout out a warning, "Timber!"

"Nona, look out!"

An instant later, one of the legion of beetle-rotted pine trees crashed to the ground right in front of us, creating a sharp, splintered barrier between the pack of dogs and their intended prey. Spirit yelped in shock and surprise, then tucked tail and ran off into the woods like a frightened pup. The rest of the dogs followed suit. Nona and I sighed our relief as we heard their yipping chorus fade off in the distance.

Exhausted, more from stress and fear than our hike through the woods, we trudged back down the mountainside in the dark with only a new moon to help light our way. Occasionally we paused, still alert for signs that our attackers might have returned. We heard nothing but the helpful wind soughing through the pines and the occasional muffled sound of pinecones dropping to the needle-strewn forest carpet below.

At last, I spotted the comforting sight of lights shining through the windows of my cabin. Home had never looked as inviting to me as it did now. I'm sure Nona and the dogs were as happy as I was when we were finally safe inside my cozy alpine abode.

"You unleash these two hounds, Nona, and I'll put on a kettle."

"Good. A hot cup of tea is just what I need after that. Where did all those stray dogs come from?"

"Escapees from Lakeside Shelter, no doubt."

"How did they escape from the shelter?"

"Someone had to have let them out, of course."

"But why? Don't they know how dangerous that could be to the public?"

"Whoever did this didn't care about that or didn't think about the consequences of 'freeing' the shelter dogs."

"I don't understand why anyone would do something like that."

"To make a point, perhaps." I saw Tori Thatcher and TAILS written all over this dog prison breakout. Who else but an activist group like hers would pull such a stunt?

"But what if they attack a child or kill someone's pet? Those animals could easily have hurt us, or Cruiser and Calamity."

"I know."

"We were lucky that rotten log fell over when it did or we'd all have been done for."

I knew that luck didn't have much to do with the tree falling when or where it did. I believed it could only have been my mother's benevolent spirit in the woods intervening for our safety. Speaking of a Spirit in the woods, we still had a big problem on our hands. A pack of feral dogs wasn't something you wanted roaming free in an area heavily populated with summer tourists. A disaster was bound to occur. The strays would have to be trapped as soon as possible before any damage was done, but that would be difficult with the animals running loose in the forest. The terrain would make it much harder for the dogcatcher to apprehend those furry fugitives. Where was Round 'em Up Rhoda when you really needed her?

Chapter 20

The articles I wrote for the *Tattler* about the break-in at the shelter and the feral dog pack we encountered in the forest were intended to alert Tahoe residents and tourists of possible danger, but it didn't prevent the inevitable from occurring. Days later, a five-year-old boy was bitten by a stray dog. Whether or not it was one of the shelter dogs or another stray wandering in the community no one knew for sure. The culprit had successfully eluded all attempts to capture him.

Fortunately, the child was only bitten on the hand, and although he did have to undergo precautionary rabies treatment, the bite was not too severe. No stitches were required, and there was no permanent damage done, except perhaps that of a psychological nature. I hated the thought of a young child being bitten by a dog, not just because of the physical injury but because he would no doubt grow up suffering from cynophobia. Someone who is afraid of dogs is one less person who is going to adopt a homeless dog, and there aren't enough homes to go around as it is. So, whoever was responsible for the shelter break-in had unleashed problems more far-reaching than a bunch of stray dogs wreaking havoc in the community.

Meanwhile, there were problems of a murderous nature still unsolved, namely, the Rhoda Marx case. The most obvious perpetrator of the crime was the same person or persons who broke into the shelter and released all the dogs. My best guess was that TAILS was wagging this dog of a case, but there was no conclusive evidence to support my hunch. The killer could be any number of people who had it in for Rhoda Marx. She certainly wasn't the most popular gal on the canine cellblock. In talking to her co-workers and even her casual acquaintances, I sensed the animosity they felt for "Mengele Marx," as she was best known to those who loathed her, and that went double for the animal lovers on the list, as I was about to discover.

"Mom, telephone for you."

"Coming. Say, have you seen my favorite earrings lying around here anywhere?"

"You mean the ruby ones Dad gave you?"
"Yes. I've lost one."
"Oh, no! Are you sure?"
"I found one of them on the nightstand, but I can't find the other one."
"I'll search while you take this call."
"Is it Skip?"
"No, Jenna Fairbanks."
"Oh, all right. I hope she isn't going to ask me to foster another crazy dog." I went to answer the phone and spotted Calamity in the living room with Cruiser. She looked as innocent as a lamb, which made me wonder what she'd been up to. When she saw me heading in the direction of the kitchen, she ceased her industrious gnawing of a rawhide chew. The only time she wasn't into some kind of mischief was when she had a chew toy to occupy her. She was still a young dog, and with her nervous nature, chewing something seemed to provide an outlet for all that pent-up energy. Cruiser had long since outgrown his need to chew. He was more into power napping when he wasn't on a crime beat with me. I was glad to see Calamity busy with something that was on my approved list of chewies. I knew it couldn't last, though. I heard the tap of toenails on hardwood as she abandoned her pacifier in the hope of acquiring something

more palatable from Cruiser's stash.

I picked up the phone, keeping a wary eye on Calamity.

"Hello."

"Hi, Elsie. How's it going?"

"All right, Jenna. And you?"

"Fine. Say, I know you're busy, but can you possibly find time to lend a hand with the preparations for our Bassetille Day event?"

She wasn't asking for me to make more room at the inn for another incorrigible basset, so who cared if there was another item added to my endless to-do list? Never mind that the one at the top of my list was a real killer.

"What do you need me to do?"

"I'm scheduling a meeting this afternoon for volunteers to form some planning committees for the event. Can you come to my house at two?"

"I'll be there. By the way, have you found anyone to adopt Calamity?"

"No, not yet. Is she giving you trouble?"

"Let's just say she's living up to her name."

"I can try to find another foster home for her if it's not working out."

"No, that's okay. It's nothing I can't manage. Maybe someone will adopt her at the

Waddle. It's only a couple of weeks away. We can last that long." I tried to keep the doubt from creeping into my voice, but Jenna picked up on it like a hound on a hunt.

"Are you certain?"

"Uh-huh. Calamity's scheduled for her first training class next week, and she's already gained some weight, so she should be looking good in time for the Waddle."

"That ought to help matters. If only people would take the time to train their dogs, fewer would end up in shelters in the first place."

I suspected that Calamity's problems went far deeper than a lack of training classes, although classes certainly would have helped. "She's a beautiful little dog, but she has some issues, as you know."

"Don't we all? I can think of a few people I know who could have used some basic training."

"So true, Jenna." That was another list of mine that seemed to grow longer all the time. We'd have to compare lists sometime. When I hung up the phone, I realized I had more company in the kitchen. While I had been talking to Jenna, Cruiser had joined Calamity in launching an all-out assault on the Yum-Yum Nook. While I was distracted, she had managed to open the cupboard door and was standing on her hind legs to reach the shelf where I kept the primo treats. I was frankly surprised that she wasn't balanced on Cruiser's back in a pantry-raiding pyramid to reach the topmost shelf. Stretched full length, her slender body reminded me of a child's Slinky toy. She snapped at empty air as she desperately tried to nab the edge of a bag of Beggin' Strips. "Calamity, no!"

She yelped her alarm and obeyed my command, but only because I had surprised her.

"Caught you in the act, didn't I? All right, you two. I'll give you a tidbit, then it's out of the kitchen with both of you."

Before I could grab the bag, it fell from the shelf and the contents spilled out on the linoleum. Quicker than a flea can jump, Calamity had gobbled up every last bacon strip. Cruiser didn't stand a chance. Who needed a Dyson "Animal" with her around to vacuum my floor?

Nona heard Calamity's yelp and came running on the double from the bedroom. She looked genuinely distressed, as though she expected to find something far worse than two dogs pillaging the pantry. I interpreted her distress as worry about me, but I couldn't have been more wrong.

"What's the matter?"

"It's just Calamity."

"I heard her cry out. Is she all right? Cruiser didn't snap at her again, did he?"

"Of course not, but I wouldn't blame him if he had. She was the one doing the snapping at Cruiser's treats."

"Maybe she's hungry."

"That dog is always hungry. If I didn't know better I'd think she had a tapeworm. Everything is fair game for Calamity. She's liable to get hold of something she shouldn't eat if we're not careful. Which reminds me, did you find my missing earring?"

"No. I looked everywhere."

"Did you check under the bed?"

"There, too. Are you sure you left them on the nightstand?"

"Yes. I always remove my earrings last thing before I go to sleep."

"Unless you lost the earring someplace else, it's bound to turn up here sooner or later."

"It's not likely I lost it elsewhere. Those earrings have a safety latch, so they don't come off easily."

"Don't worry, Mom. I'll keep an eye out for it. I know how much they mean to you."

"Can you stick around this afternoon? I have to go to a meeting, and I'd rather not leave the dogs unattended, especially you-know-who."

"Sure, I can stay with them. I don't have any plans except for some reading I want to catch up on."

"Thanks, honey. I shouldn't be too long."

"Take your time. We'll be fine." I always felt bad about asking Nona to dog-sit whenever she came up to visit me. Despite her affection for Cruiser, she hadn't acted very enthusiastic about it in the past, but something was different this time. I expected her to be out on a manhunt, like she usually is when she comes to Tahoe, but she preferred hanging around the cabin with the dogs and me this time. I hoped it wasn't because Nona was sicker than she was letting on. We never talk about health issues much. Neither of us likes to complain about our aches and pains or likes hearing about them, either. Until now neither of us ever had anything much to complain about. It was obvious that she seemed to enjoy being around Calamity. Was it because Calamity was fiercely independent and kind of a wild child like Nona? Or was my daughter finally becoming a dog person like her mother? Whatever the reason for the change in Nona, I had to give at least some credit to Calamity, doggone her mischievous hide.

Chapter 21

Jenna's place was located near Fallen Leaf Lake, not far from where my ancestral home once stood before it was destroyed in a forest fire. Her house didn't look much different than ours had, with its rustic rock fireplace and foundation. Driving down the long road that meandered through the pines and aspen groves, I pulled off the road a moment to admire the lake, one of several smaller bodies of water surrounding Lake Tahoe that were formed eons ago in this alpine region.

Like the other lakes, Fallen Leaf was not without its rich collection of legends and lore. Author John Steinbeck and numerous others who have found creative inspiration beside the various lakes of this region had traversed the potholed road I jostled down now. Some people think Fallen Leaf Lake was so named because of its distinctive shape, but when viewed from the summit of

Mount Tallac, the nearly four-mile-long body of water, which appears as richly sapphire in hue as the bigger lake and is situated eighty feet higher in elevation, more closely resembles the shape of a human foot. Ancient man might have thought some giant creature left its footprint here, which later filled with water to create the lake.

I passed the ruins of Anita Baldwin's rustic cabin on the two thousand acres she inherited from her father, Comstock millionaire Lucky Baldwin, along with half his twenty million-dollar estate, when he died in 1909. Photographer Dorothea Lange summered there with her family. While the children who came along with Dorothea and her husband ran around wild and naked all summer on the secluded property, pretending to be Indians in the sweat house the family built while they were visiting, Dorothea busied herself shooting forms of nature — pine trees, stumps, and the golden sunlight filtering through broad leaves — though she achieved her fame from photographing people during the Great Depression.

None of Fallen Leaf Lake's history was as rich in my mind as the Tahoe history of my own family. The idyllic summers of Steinbeck, Baldwin, and Lange held no power over the memory of ours. I looked back with fondness and bittersweet longing upon all the happy times we spent there together each summer when my grandparents and parents were still living. I remembered fishing with my grandfather beside the lake, catching trout by the boatload. I could see the rainbow-striped scales of the fish glistening in the sun as they danced on the end of the line. Somewhere deep inside, I was still that little pigtailed girl who delighted in wading in the shallows and leaping from stone to stone. I could almost feel the cool, smooth rocks of the lake bed beneath my bare feet.

I recalled the time I was wading in the lake and slipped on some mossy stones. Next thing I knew, I was underwater. When I surfaced for air, looking like a drowned rat in my soaking wet clothes, I realized that my mother was filming the event for posterity with her movie camera, laughing her head off. At least I know where I get my warped sense of humor. Looking back on it now, I have to admit it was pretty funny. That was a lifetime ago, but the memories are still as verdant in my mind as the summer greenery that surrounds this hidden lake.

Jenna met me at the front door before I

could ring the bell.

"Beanie, come on in. We've been waiting for you."

"Sorry. I got a little sidetracked on the way here."

"That's okay. I was just making some coffee. I think you already know everyone, except for my good friend, Roberta Finch. Everyone calls her Bertie."

"We haven't actually met before."

"I'll let you go ahead and introduce yourselves while I finish up in the kitchen."

Even TAILS couldn't have boasted a collection of any more dedicated animal advocates than were assembled in Jenna Fairbanks's spacious living room, which was occupied by another collection of rescued canines and felines. Now I understood why she hadn't let me ring the doorbell. Chaos would surely have ensued. Several bassets, mostly hard-to-place seniors, snoozed comfortably in fleece snuggly beds. The cats made themselves comfortable wherever they wanted. I hoped the kitchen was off limits. I don't care for cat hair in my coffee. Dog hair is okay, of course. Jenna's home was considerably roomier for housing rescues than my two-dog-capacity cabin, although it had accommodated three on occasion.

Besides Jenna, who along with Bertie was

the driving force behind this Bassetille Day event, Amanda Peabody and Cruiser's and my old friend, Sally Applebaum from the Haute Hydrant pet store, were there. Amanda was in charge of games and contests for the dogs, and Sally was to provide the contest prizes and solicit donations of items for the silent auction. Since I was the only writer in the group, it wasn't hard to guess who was to be in charge of advertising and promotion. Bertie had volunteered to handle any adoptions of homeless hounds at the Waddle. In fact, she had insisted on it, and everyone understood the reason why. It was Bertie's dog, Gilda, who had been tragically killed before she could be redeemed from Lakeside Shelter, despite the fact that she was microchipped. Gilda had become the cause célèbre of this fundraiser. Everyone blamed Rhoda Marx and her rigid pound policies for the dog's needless death. Bertie was still furious about it.

Jenna returned from the kitchen with the coffee and poured us each a cup.

"What kind of turnout are you expecting for our event?" I asked her.

"We've got about three hundred people registered so far. Your online ads have really helped get the word out."

"That's a decent number for our small

community."

"I doubt we'll have the kind of attendance they do at some Basset Waddles, like the ones held in Michigan and Illinois, but people will travel a long way to waddle with the bassets. We have several registrants from Canada, and even a few from abroad."

"I'm sure the location of our waddle is an added attraction. People from all over the world come to visit Lake Tahoe."

"How are we doing on donations for the silent auction, Sally?" Jenna said.

"People have been very generous so far. We've had a lot of support from Petropolis and other businesses in the area."

"I guess we aren't the only ones who want to see Tahoe have a state-of-the-art animal shelter," I said.

"The sooner that terrible place is demolished, the better," Bertie said. "Gilda's spirit won't rest until every last rotten brick of it is razed to the ground."

"I'm so sorry about your dog," I said. "It was such a terrible tragedy."

"Delicious coffee cake, Jenna," Sally said. "You must give me the recipe."

"Of course. Happy to. It was my mother's favorite."

I noticed Sally giving me a funny look. I realized that she and Jenna were trying their best to change the subject, but it was too late. I'd evidently said the wrong thing. The floodgates opened.

Bertie began to sob uncontrollably. "My poor, poor Gilda. I'll never get over losing her. Never!"

"I'm so sorry. I shouldn't have brought it up."

"No, I'm glad you did."

"How did she end up in the pound, anyway?"

"I was called away on a family emergency, and my neighbor, who was watching her, accidentally let her get out. Gilda was a wanderer, so you had to watch her very carefully or she'd give you the slip when your back was turned."

"Most people don't know the nature of these hounds," I said. "They'll follow that keen nose anywhere. That's how we ended up with Cruiser. He was wandering loose on the streets when my husband saw him. If Tom hadn't found him, I don't think Cruiser would have had a happy ending, either. I still have to watch him when he's off leash or he'll do his famous disappearing act."

"Gilda had a microchip. There was no need for my darling girl to end up the way she did. She wasn't sick or homeless. That evil Rhoda Marx killed her, and I'm glad she ended up the same way all her helpless victims did."

"I know you're still hurting over Gilda's loss, but that sounds pretty cold-hearted, Bertie," Jenna said to her grieving friend.

"No colder than that horrid woman was, and you know it, Jenna. She deserved the same treatment she gave so many innocent animals that could have found homes if they'd only been given half a chance."

No one here was going to disagree with that statement. The room was dead silent, except for the sound of snoring bassets. It was what Bertie said next that gave us all cause for concern about her state of mind.

"Care for some more coffee, Bertie?" Jenna asked.

"No, I'd better not. I haven't been sleeping well lately."

"You, too?" I said. "Those night sweats are murder."

"No, it's not that. It's Gilda."

"Oh, did she used to sleep with you?" Amanda said. "I can't sleep a wink without my canine comforters, either."

"Me, neither," I said. "Even if Cruiser snores. A snoring dog is white noise for a dog lover, though. Lulls me to sleep every time."

"You don't understand," Bertie said. "Something wakes me up every night. I feel a pressure on my chest."

"You should see a doctor, Bertie." Jenna said.

"Gosh, that sounds like there could be something wrong with your heart," Sally said.

"There's something wrong with my heart, all right. It's been broken to bits. But what I'm feeling is nothing like that. It feels like a pair of paws resting on my chest. That's what Gilda used to do. Sometimes, if I was having a restless night, she would crawl up in the middle of the night and place her paws gently upon my chest, and she always did the same thing every morning to wake me."

"You must just be dreaming, dear," Jenna said.

"It's no dream. I'm fully awake when it happens. I know it's Gilda's ghost. I've even seen her! She's come back to haunt me for letting her die." Bertie buried her face in her hands. It was hard watching someone suffer so over the loss of her pet.

"Oh, Bertie, please don't do this to yourself. You didn't let her die. It was an accident. I know you're distraught over her death, but you have to stop grieving so for her. Gilda wouldn't want you to be in such pain. She loved you too much to ever want you to hurt this much."

Bertie looked up at Jenna and then at the rest of us. I don't know what emotion was registering on my face, but I hope I didn't seem as patronizing as the rest of the women in our group.

"I know you all think I'm insane, but I know what I saw. I didn't imagine it. Gilda has come back, and her ghost will never rest until Lakeside Shelter and everyone who had anything to do with her death is history." With that Bertie abruptly stood up. In so doing, she spilled her coffee all over Jenna's coffee table. She didn't pause to apologize but stormed out the front door. The sound of the door slamming woke up the snoring bassets.

We were all dumbfounded until I finally said, "I guess this meeting is officially adjourned."

Chapter 22

Driving home from the committee meeting, I kept thinking about what Roberta Finch had said about Gilda. Was she having worse menopausal symptoms than most women her age, a candidate for the nearest psych ward, or had she really experienced a hound haunting? I have heard of people who have recently lost a beloved pet claiming to have heard the sounds of toenails clicking on the floor or the jangling of dog tags. Some feel Fuzzy the cat circling their ankles, as it would have when it heard the sound of the can opener at feeding time.

Others claim to experience the sensation of the bed's edge dipping as though the animal is climbing up as it did in life, and the same thing Bertie felt, paws pressing upon her chest. It's not that uncommon for people to claim they see an apparition of their pet after it has passed. Whether this is all wishful thinking on the part of grieving pet owners or whether the animal's spirit really does come back to visit the human it was so devoted to in life is certainly debatable, but I have no doubt that every animal has a spirit, like any other living, breathing creature.

Who's to say where that spirit goes after death? If for some reason the animal's spirit is not at rest, it's not unreasonable to believe that it could come back to comfort its owner as it did in life, or perhaps even help that owner avenge its untimely death, as in Gilda's case. It was clear Gilda's owner had no doubts about that.

What concerned me even more than Bertie's obvious distress over the tragic loss of Gilda was her animosity toward the person who was responsible for her demise, Rhoda Marx. From everything I'd heard thus far, it was clear that no one liked Rhoda, but Bertie's feelings went far beyond dislike. We'd all heard her say she was glad Rhoda was dead and that she died the way she did. I suppose I might say the same thing about anyone who hurt my dog. I don't think I'd go as far as someone had to get even with Rhoda Marx, but Bertie's enmity toward Rhoda begged the question, Had she somehow been involved in her death?

■ ■ ■ ■

I was met at my front door first by Cruiser and then by Calamity, who charged past him to greet me, probably because she smelled traces of other bassets and the lingering aroma of Jenna's yummy coffee cake on my clothes. That move was a big mistake on the newcomer's part, because Cruiser quickly put her in her place as only an alpha dog can. He whirled on Calamity, let out a gruff admonition and gave her a good gumming on the ruff of her neck. Calamity cried out her surprise at Cruiser's unexpected reprisal. There was no harm done to her except for a generous dousing of slobber, but she got the message right away. The rule of the pack is supreme, even for the normally laidback basset hound. So far, Cruiser had been more successful at behavior modification with Calamity than either Nona or I. We might have to recruit Cruiser as her trainer.

"How did your meeting go?" Nona said.

"It didn't. We didn't accomplish very much this afternoon. We kind of got off track."

"I know how that goes. It's hard to keep meetings focused sometimes."

"Oh, this one was focused, all right. It just wasn't what I expected we'd be focused on."

"Which was?"

"One of the ladies was very upset about her dog." I didn't go into more detail. I didn't want to get into further discussion of the Rhoda Marx case with Nona for the moment. Besides, I could tell from her tone of voice that something was amiss on the home front and needed my immediate attention. I was right.

"I think you'll be very upset with your dog when you find out what she's been up to, Mom."

"Calamity is not *my* dog." That was wishful thinking on my part. Potential adopters weren't exactly beating down my front door to take her off my hands. I was almost afraid to ask my next question. "What's she done now?"

"Come with me. I'll show you."

I followed Nona to my bedroom, fearing what I was about to discover when I opened the door. I'd certainly taken on a load of trouble when I agreed to foster Crazy Calamity, and with a murderer still on the loose, there was already plenty of trouble to go around.

Calamity followed close on our heels, but she turned tail and shot back down the hall when she heard the ire rise in my voice as I gazed at the canine crime scene that lay before me. My white duvet was smeared top to bottom with stains. It was like one of those paw paintings you see at animal rescue benefits. "What's that brown stuff all over my duvet?" I wasn't sure I really wanted to know.

"It's chocolate."

"Chocolate! Where did she get chocolate?" Around my house that was like asking where Willy Wonka hides his golden tickets. There was always a stash of chocolate hidden somewhere on the MacBean property, if you knew where to look. Sometimes I hid my treats so well I forgot where I put them myself. Calamity had evidently discovered my private reserve. She was so good at breaking and entering that lockbox, which held not only Cruiser's goodies but also mine, I was surprised she hadn't been able to spring herself free from Lakeside Shelter.

"Apparently, Cruiser's treats weren't good enough for her. She went for yours instead." Nona tried not to laugh when she said it but couldn't contain herself. She burst out laughing at the Jackson Pollock–inspired painted canvas that was once my bedspread.

"This is no laughing matter, Nona. Chocolate is harmful to dogs, and it looks like Calamity got a pretty good dose of it here. Chocolate has theobromine in it, and there's more of it in dark chocolate like this. It can kill a dog if they get too much in their system."

"How would you know if they got too much?"

"The dog would act agitated, for one thing."

"How could you tell with Calamity? She's always agitated."

"Point taken. This dog has a stomach of iron, but I think I'd better get her to the vet right away, just in case."

"I'm afraid she has something else in her system, too."

"What?"

"I finally figured out what happened to your earring."

"You did? What?"

"Calamity has been eating our earrings. She ate mine, too."

"How do you know?"

"I found some that had obviously been gnawed. A few of the mates are missing, so I can pretty much guess where they went. She must have gotten into my travel case."

About that time, I heard a suspicious noise down the hall in the kitchen. Calamity was probably back in the pantry looking for something else to get into. I caught her before she nabbed a whole box of Ding Dongs.

"No you don't, young lady! It's off to Doc Heaton with you." I snapped on her leash and hurried out the door with Calamity, her muzzle still smeared with the evidence of her latest escapade. Evidently, there was more than one chocoholic residing at the MacBean cabin.

Chapter 23

If I thought life with Calamity couldn't get any more difficult, I was wrong, as I was about to discover on our next visit to the veterinarian. Why do dogs always seem to know when you are taking them to the vet? Calamity had been to Doc Heaton's clinic only once before, but the moment I turned the car into the parking lot, she freaked out, bouncing around the car like she was spring loaded. It could also have been the chocolate in her system causing such extreme behavior, but since she had already yarked up most of the offending substance on my living room carpet before we left the house, I doubted that was entirely the case. I know chocolate is harmful for dogs, and I thought I had put my stash in a dogproof place, but it was hard to put things far enough out of reach to keep them from Calamity's greedy little paws. I kept thinking, "Why did it have to be my expensive gourmet Godiva chocolates and not the Hershey's candy bars I sometimes carry in my purse?" Fortunately for her, she hadn't gotten into my dark baking chocolate, which would have been more harmful and possibly deadly. It doesn't take much of that to kill a dog. Calamity's size was also in her favor. The dose she got could quickly have killed a smaller dog, but I had no doubt I was going to have this crazy hound around for a while to come.

As I dragged Calamity into the veterinarian's office, she actually latched onto the doorjamb with her front paws like a willful child. I was engaged in a kind of canine taffy pull and fast losing the battle with the belligerent basset until one of the vet techs intervened. She gave Calamity a shot of sedative to calm her down so that the staff could do an ultrasound on her and treat her for the chocolate overdose, if need be.

I waited in the examining room for what seemed like hours while Calamity was being treated. I realized that I was waiting in the same room as when I nearly lost Cruiser to poisoning of another kind during the Sirius case. I still had bad memories of that terrible day. The prospect of life without Cruiser was too horrible to imagine. Doc Heaton had been put through his professional paces on that case. Cruiser's guardian angel also lent a helping paw. I found myself feeling almost as worried about Calamity's welfare now as I had then about Cruiser's.

I hated to admit it, but this dog was starting to grow on me in spite of my every effort not to become too attached to a foster dog. Not as much as she was growing on Nona, even though I knew my daughter was enough like her father to not want to admit her sympathy and increasing affection for a homeless dog. Calamity needed a friend, and she was fast finding one in Nona. The fact that she slept with Nona at night was conclusive enough evidence to me that their bond was becoming stronger with each passing day. I knew Nona was worried about Calamity too, and she had wanted to come with me to the vet. I was wishing now that I had brought her along to help me with the dog, but I was fairly confident Calamity hadn't devoured enough of my chocolates to do her any permanent harm. I also wanted someone to watch Cruiser for me while I was away. Although he was no longer a curious pup inclined to chew things he shouldn't, it wasn't unknown for him to get into his own brand of mischief when left to his own devices for too long.

I had run out of pet magazines to read

and veterinary wall charts of dog and cat anatomy and canine periodontal disease to study when the door to the waiting room finally opened and a groggy Calamity ambled in, led by Doctor Heaton.

"How is she, Doc?"

"Fine. Fortunately, she didn't ingest enough chocolate to do her any lasting damage. We gave her some fluids and did a gastric lavage to get the rest of the stuff out of her. She should be back to her old self as soon as the sedative wears off."

"You couldn't send some of that sedative home with me, could you? This is the calmest she's been since I brought her home from the shelter."

Doc Heaton laughed.

"Did the ultrasound show anything?"

"Nope. It was all clear. Not a diamond earring or tiara in sight. Apparently, whatever she swallowed went straight through her system without any snags. Better keep this material girl out of your jewelry box from now on, though."

"Don't worry, I will. I'm not planning to have multiple piercings on those long ears of hers to accommodate all my earrings." I thought of Tori Thatcher's piercings. "Now that would be a sight, wouldn't it?"

"Sure would. I think once this little girl

gets settled someplace permanent and has a few training sessions, she'll calm down and stop causing so much trouble." I knew from his smile that he was hinting I should adopt Calamity, but he didn't know her like I did.

"I hope so, Doc. She's a real handful. My daughter has promised to take her to her first training class next week."

"You're a lucky girl," Doc Heaton said, giving his patient a friendly pat on her rump. "If cats have nine lives, you must have at least half that number working in your favor. Not many animals at Lakeside Shelter have been as fortunate as you."

"That's for sure," I said. "She is certainly a lot luckier than Roberta Finch's basset."

"Yes, Gilda was a patient of mine. I was very upset with the manager of the shelter over that unfortunate incident."

"So was her owner. Still is."

"I microchipped Gilda myself, so all they needed to do was scan the dog for the presence of a chip to identify her owner. The dog's death was unnecessary and inexcusable."

Doc Heaton was visibly upset. I couldn't ever remember seeing him so emotional about one of his patients, except for when we nearly lost Cruiser. Normally, he seemed rather detached. I suppose it's something you have to do in his line of work, or you'd have a hard time doing your job day in and day out. Kind of like Skip and what he encounters in the line of duty. I'd never have made it as a veterinarian. Perhaps in my next life.

"Did you know Rhoda Marx well?" I asked.

"I did a lot of the spays and neuters at the shelter for the lucky few that were claimed in time. I knew her well enough to know she was in the wrong line of work."

"From what I've heard about her, she might have been of more use at Gitmo than at Lakeside. She ran the shelter like a prisoner of war camp, according to her staff."

"Between you and me, Beanie, I was trying to persuade the city council to get rid of her before she could do any more damage. She was bad news for the entire animal care community, and the community in general. That kind of PR isn't good for Tahoe. The council was about to take action, but apparently someone saved them the trouble."

"Apparently." The question still was, who?

Day was done by the time we left Doc Heaton's office. The drive back home with Calamity was much quieter than the one on the way to the vet's office. She didn't fight my putting her in her carrier this time. The moment she was inside she curled up and fell asleep. I would gladly have slipped Doc Heaton a few bucks under the examining table for some of that miracle potion of his. For the first time, Calamity was acting like a normal basset hound. Like Cruiser, she was now calm and laid-back. Of course, I knew it couldn't last, and I wouldn't seriously keep the dog drugged to live peacefully with her, but I planned to enjoy this peace and quiet while I could. Calamity didn't even wake up when I steered the car into my driveway. Only when I opened her carrier door did she open her bloodshot eyes, which I would swear were more chocolate brown in color than they were before the infamous Godiva escapade. She'd been lucky this time, but I'd have to be much more watchful of this naughty dog in the future. I wanted her to survive long enough to find her a new home.

I could tell Nona was happy to see us come in the front door. She greeted Calamity first, who gave her a gentle lick on the hand, instead of trying to climb all over her, as she usually did.

"Are you sure this is the same dog you left here with? What did the vet do, clone her? She's so sedate."

"Exactly. She's sedated, so don't get used to this new version of Calamity. I expect the old one will return to us soon enough after the drug wears off."

"She's going to be okay, right?"

"Yes, she was lucky this time. I must be more careful in the future where I store my chocolate, though, and everything else she shouldn't get into."

Calm Calamity lay down at Nona's feet and rolled over on her back to receive a tummy rub. Nona was happy to oblige.

"Did Doc Heaton find any of our earrings in here?" Nona said, stroking Calamity's soft, white belly.

"The ultrasound was clear. No sign of any missing jewelry."

"I think I may have found some of it out in the yard, Mom."

"You did? Where?"

"Guess."

I didn't really have to guess. After talking to Doc Heaton, I already suspected where I would find the mate to my precious ruby earrings Tom gave me on our twenty-fifth wedding anniversary. Sure enough, when I followed Nona outside, there among the pine needles, glinting in the sun was The Jewel of the Pile. I'll spare you the details of our treasure hunt, but suffice to say that Nona and I got our jewelry back and after a thorough sanitizing, most of it was as good as new.

CHAPTER 24

Calamity didn't even blink when the phone rang that evening. She was still conked out from her ordeal at the vet's office. Lying side by side with Cruiser on the living room rug, they looked like bookends. This was something of a breakthrough because Cruiser hadn't tolerated her in close proximity to him until now. But when she lay down beside him, there had been no signs of disapproval from the top dog. He looked up once when she flopped down beside him and then resumed snoring. Perhaps he sensed the ordeal she'd been through at the vet, or maybe it was simply resignation that she was one of the MacBean pack, at least for now. Both dogs must have been chasing the same rabbit in their dreams because their paws paddled in unison. Synchronized swimmers could never outstroke these two.

Who knows what dogs really dream about? We assume they chase rabbits or squirrels in some verdant field of their subconscious, but with rescued dogs like Cruiser and Calamity, one never knows what terrors they might actually be fleeing from in their slumber. Are they escaping monster cats with foot-long razor-sharp claws, or Dr. FrankenHeaton wielding giant hypodermic needles? Unless I am reincarnated as a dog in my next life, I'll never know for certain, but if I am I hope I come back as an adored, spoiled hound like Cruiser. What a cushy life that would be!

When I answered the phone, Carla Meeks from the *Tattler* was on the other end of the line.

"Hey, Carla. What's up?"

"I have an assignment for you if you want it. I need someone to cover the town hall meeting tomorrow night. They'll be discussing proposed changes at Lakeside Shelter. Interested?"

"Sure am."

"Great! I'll expect an article draft by the end of the week. Deliver it sooner, and I'll add a bonus to your usual fee."

"Done." It was high time I'd been offered a raise at the *Tattler.* Actually, considering the current economic downturn and the effects of computer technology on the printed word, Carla was being very generous by offering me more money for this assignment. I suppose it was mostly because I had been writing for the *Tattler* such a long time. Also, she figured I might be retiring from reporting one of these days, and she wanted to keep writers she could depend on to deliver the goods on a tight deadline.

This job couldn't have come along at a better time for me. Not only would I have some extra income, but I'd have a front-row seat in the shelter dispute. With any luck, this controversial event might even draw Rhoda Marx's murderer out of the woods. It was certain that anyone who had any investment, either monetary or emotional, in this hot-button shelter issue in our community would be present. It wasn't quite the same as the killer returning to the scene of the crime, but it was close enough.

My clothes reeked of sweat from the backyard excavation for lost treasure along with that unique mixture of disinfectant, flea spray, and frantic pets at the vet clinic. Although most dog people wouldn't mind the aroma, it was quite a pungent blend, and I doubted it would ever be bottled for sale to the public at large. Of course, I'm still eagerly waiting for Victoria Stillwell or some other celebrity dog trainer to design her own signature fragrance and call it *Puppy Breath.* Forget Liz Taylor's White Diamonds or Chanel. There would probably never be any fragrance manufactured that could capture the essence of another Victoria I had come to know of late. A perfume called Purple and Pierced? For some perhaps, but not for *moi.*

I'd immerse myself in canine cologne that was named for the essence of puppies. For a dog lover like me, there's no aroma on earth that compares to the incomparably innocent odor of a pup's moist, slightly sour, milky breath. When you hold a tiny puppy in your hands and he puffs his momma's milk scent of unconditional love into your face to be inhaled and savored, nothing is sweeter. Perhaps it's even sweeter because that innocence of puppyhood is so quickly and completely lost, never to be regained. It's a love they know only for eight weeks of their life, sometimes even less, but despite what people may think, I believe it's a love they remember forever. If you have ever watched a dreaming adult dog suckle in its dreams, even when it's very old, you know this to be true.

No one ever forgets Mother, and Mother never forgets us. She never stops loving us as long as she lives, no matter how old we are. I suspect the same is true of dogs, which gives one pause when you consider that we separate puppies from their mothers so young, often far too young. I had no doubt that this might have been part of Calamity's behavior problems and could keep her from ever being a well-adjusted member of anyone's household. Whenever I wore my Puppy Breath out on the town for any occasion, I would really be wearing a mother's enduring love for her offspring. It's the same way I feel about my own offspring, so perhaps I'd just have to come up with a uniquely lovely fragrance of my own creation one day and call it Nona.

With Skip coming over later for supper, I didn't want to overwhelm him with my current essence of D.O. (Doggy Odor), so I decided I'd better shower and tidy up. This particular aroma, mixed with my spicy chili and garlic bread, would probably take anyone's appetite, even that die-hard bean eater, Skip's.

Chapter 25

Anytime I served my chili, Skip had a standing invitation to join me for dinner. He was late arriving tonight, which wasn't like him. Skip is never late for a free meal if he can help it. When I saw him, I understood why he was tardy this time.

"Gosh, Skip. You look whipped. Been working double shifts or something?"

"Something like that. How'd you know?"

"From the dark circles under your eyes."

"I haven't been sleeping much at night."

"You look like you've been dipped in gunpowder."

"That would be Cannon fodder."

"Oh, you mean your partner, Rusty?"

"Yes, her."

"Problems with the new recruit?"

"And how! Say, you got any beer in the fridge?"

"Sure. I'll go get you one."

"One'll do for starters."

Our conversation had aroused Cruiser and Calamity from their slumbers. Cruiser waddled over and greeted Skip with his usual basset hound version of enthusiasm, and Calamity followed suit. I could tell that some comforting canine attention was just what my friend needed. I knew from personal experience that it's all anyone needs when life is getting you down. That and chocolate.

Calamity nudged Skip's hand, and he stroked her head. "Did you take in another rescue?"

"No, it's the same one."

"Really? I'd never have guessed. She certainly seems a lot calmer than the last time I saw her. I had to practically pry her off me before."

"You and everyone else."

"Those dog trainers are miracle workers."

"Doc Heaton is the miracle worker, but it's only a temporary miracle, I'm afraid. She's still sedated from her emergency visit at the vet's."

"Uh-oh. What happened?"

"We had a little mishap with some chocolate. She's fine now, though."

"That's good. Whatever he gave her sure made a different dog out of her."

"Yeah, Nona asked me if she was a Calamity clone."

Skip laughed and took a swig of his brew. I could see him starting to loosen up. Beer was apparently a good sedative, too.

"I doubt that the effects will last, unfortunately. I expect we'll have the same old troublesome girl back soon."

The mention of trouble swept the smile off Skip's face. Something was wrong. I hoped he felt he could confide in me. After all, what are friends for besides killer chili and cold beer, and occasionally saving your life?

"I can tell something's bothering you, Skip. Feel like talking about it?"

He took another long slug of cold draft before answering. "Rusty has accused me and others in the department of discrimination."

"That's not good."

"No, it's not. It gets worse, though."

"How so?"

"She also threatened to slap us with a sexual harassment lawsuit."

"You're right. That's a lot worse."

"She may have to go on administrative leave until this is resolved. I should never have hired her in the first place. Even Cruiser could have smelled she was trouble from the get-go. Note to self: Never hire a centerfold."

"You don't know whether there might be extenuating circumstances that forced her to earn extra cash. Maybe she has a sick mother to support or something."

"It doesn't matter. She's an officer of the law, and it's inappropriate for her to be moonlighting in the sex industry. If she wants to do that kind of work, she can get a job at Mustang Ranch. She'd probably earn more there, anyway, than she does at the sheriff's office."

"Come on now, Skip. Why is she making these accusations? You didn't hang that pin-up of her in your locker after all, did you?" I was trying to lighten him up, but it wasn't working tonight.

"No, I didn't, but some of the other guys got another one and did. She claims they've been hitting on her, too."

"Not too surprising. She's an attractive gal, and that uniform of hers is pretty form-fitting, but she wasn't wearing it in her *Playboy* spread. Anyway, I'm sure it's not the first time she's been hit on."

"Maybe not, but she's an officer too, and they should know better."

"What did you do to her, though?"

"She thinks I'm holding her back professionally because she's a female and . . . well, you know."

"A former stripper?"

"Yeah. I don't think I've treated her any different than I would any other officer on the force."

"She's a female in a traditionally male profession. That automatically puts her at a disadvantage."

"I think it's mostly her inexperience that's holding her back, not anything she claims I've done."

"What did she say to you?"

"She said her only regret was that she didn't do it sooner. She's made a bundle from her exposure, so to speak. She's even had a couple of movie offers, but she didn't say what kind of roles she's been offered."

"Being beautiful can be a blessing or a curse for a woman. Just ask Nona. She's had to deal with some of the same issues in her profession. That glass ceiling may have some cracks, but it's still not broken. Nice girls finish last, and sometimes we have to break a few rules to get where we're going. A woman nearly made it to the White House, but we still have a long way to go before we're Queen of the Hill."

"Where is Nona tonight, anyway?"

"She went to the Washoe Health Center."

"What for?"

"She's getting a second opinion from them."

"Opinion about what?"

"She probably would be furious at me for talking about this to you behind her back, but Nona has had a suspicious mammogram."

"Oh."

"Her grandmother died of breast cancer, and those things often skip a generation, so it's got me plenty worried."

"I'm sure."

"I try not to show it for her sake, though."

"Probably for the best."

I could see Skip was uncomfortable talking about breasts, unless they were bared on a pin-up girl. Most men have trouble expressing themselves about personal problems, particularly if they have to do with "womany stuff." I did us both a favor and changed the subject back to helping him solve his problems, which suited him just fine.

"What are you going to do about the trouble you're having with Rusty?"

"I'm not sure. I've gone out of my way to be nice to her and make things as easy as possible for her."

"Maybe that's the trouble. She didn't seem like the kind of gal who would appreciate preferential treatment, especially from a man. She probably finds it condescending. If she joined the force, that means she wants to play hardball with the boys, not be handled with kid gloves."

"You may be right. Anyway, it's out of my hands now. This is one for internal affairs. I'm glad because I have problems of my own with this Marx murder case still unsolved. We really don't have much to go on thus far. The only prints we lifted from the crime scene were canine."

"What else would you expect to find at a dog pound?"

We laughed, but we both knew it was no laughing matter. There was a killer on the loose, and until he or she was collared, no one could rest easy, except maybe for those lazy bassets, Cruiser and Calamity, who had gone back to whatever bad guys they chased in their dog dreams. If only it were that easy chasing bad guys for real.

Chapter 26

Skip didn't stay long after he downed his chili and beer. Ordinarily, he wouldn't eat and run, but I knew he had a lot more on his plate than my chili. Not long after he left, Nona got home. Calamity's head popped up. She already recognized the sound of Nona's car engine, like Cruiser knows the sound of mine. She got up and moseyed toward the front door, apparently still a bit loopy from her visit to the vet. Cruiser looked up briefly and resumed his nap. He figured Calamity had the doorbell covered this time. There were some advantages to having another dog in the household. That meant he didn't have to jump up every time the door needed answering.

"Hey, Calamity. How're you feeling, girl?" Nona knelt down to greet the young dog, something she never would have done before, especially if any drool were involved. She didn't seem to mind the saliva from

Calamity's lip folds that smeared on her forearm. "She still looks a bit doped, doesn't she, Mom?"

"Yeah, with eyes as bloodshot as hers, I'm surprised Skip didn't throw her in the drunk tank for the night to sleep it off."

"I saw him leaving as I drove up. From the aroma in here, I'm guessing he came over for some chili, huh?"

"What else?"

"He didn't stay very long."

"I know. He has a lot going on at the office. How was your visit at the health center?"

"Fine. It was a little different than I was expecting."

"What were you expecting?"

"I don't know. I guess because it's tribal I thought it was going to be all primitive and everything, but it's really more of a blend of old and new medicine, from a Native perspective. I like that."

"Good, honey. I'm glad you'll be comfortable with the treatment you'll receive there."

"They suggested I visit a Native American Church, but I don't even know what that is. You know I've never been very 'churchy.' "

"I never liked the White Man's churches."

"I know. The only time I've been in a church was for Dad's funeral. Would you come along with me?"

"Of course."

I knew Nona would get some good medicine in our people's church. So would I. She wasn't the only one who needed to chase away some evil spirits, especially with all this murder on my mind.

I never brought Nona up in any kind of church and was never much of a churchgoer myself, even though Tom was Presbyterian and would have liked me to join him on Sundays. I felt out of place in the White Man's church. Still do. My church doesn't have four walls. It is out in nature. Why would I want to be inside a stuffy building when I can be under the wide-open sky inhaling the scent of pines and listening to the wind talk among the branches? No sermon can move me like that, nor can any pipe organ chords compare with the chorus of birds and woodland creatures and water burbling over stones in mountain streams. The light from candles cannot match the light of the sun reflected on the surface of the lake or stars strewn like rare diamonds across a black velvet night.

No, the White Man's religion never had much appeal for our people, even though Whites have spent a lot of time and spilled a lot of blood trying to convert Native Americans to their beliefs. Whites still don't like us practicing our Indian ways, and they sure don't like the Native American Church, where many of our tribe worships. They even passed laws to keep us from going to our church to practice our own religion. So far, the local law had turned a blind eye to our sacred ceremonies, thanks mostly to my friend who is also the county sheriff.

Religion's a personal thing, in my way of thinking, and it's not right to impose your own beliefs on anyone else. Who's to say that one person's way of connecting to God or Spirit or whatever you want to call it is any more right than another? Like up here in the mountains, there are many trails a man can follow to reach the same summit. So I chose not to push religion of any kind on my daughter while she was growing up, leaving her to choose her own, or not.

This wasn't my first time in the Native American Church, but it would be Nona's. Like a lot of the young people in her generation, she isn't much interested in learning the old ways. Whether it was hope or mere curiosity on her part, she wanted to join the ceremony. In fact, she was the main reason for this meeting. The people were coming together not just to sit in the circle and sing.

There was work to do. We had come here to pray in a healing ceremony for my daughter, and she was open to that.

We decided to meet in a secluded area where there would be no likelihood of intruders. As Sonseah requested, I hadn't told anyone outside the tribe about our assembly. She didn't want to attract the wrong attention. I didn't even tell Skip about it. Some locals might decide to take an exception to our prayer meetings because of the medicine we use in the ceremony, so I didn't want to put Skip in a tight spot with the sheriff's department. He had enough troubles to deal with right now. Washoe have the legal right to use the medicine in the practice of their religion, but anyone else might end up in jail for using it. That's kind of funny to us Indians since God created the medicine for us, and we've been using it for all kinds of purposes for thousands of years, long before the Whites ever set foot on our land.

It was nightfall when we gathered for the ceremony. The deerskin of the tipi glowed ghostly white in the light of the full moon that crested the eastern ridge of the Sierra. One could almost believe that the spirit of the animal that gave up its hide for the tipi still inhabited it. Most Native American

Churches have only canvas instead of deer or buffalo skins, but our chief, Dan Silvernail, has the real thing.

My grandfather was also a tribal chief in his time. He'd had a tipi that was made from an animal that lived many generations ago, and it was passed down to him from his grandfather. That was in the days when our animal brethren were much more abundant in Tahoe, and there weren't so many rules telling the Washoe that they couldn't freely hunt them. The Indians were never greedy and cruel like the Whites, though, killing animals merely for sport or profit. We never stacked up heaps of carcasses like they did the plains buffalo, wolves, and other animals for the price of their pelts while Indians starved and froze. When we killed an animal, it was for a good reason, for food or clothing or shelter or to survive. Or for use in the practice of our religion. We always honored the animal that gave up its life to keep us alive. No animal ever died in vain.

Dan and his helpers had made sure everything was prepared for the meeting. First they raised the four big poles of the tipi and bound them together. North, south, east and west poles symbolize the unity of all the races on Earth and that we'll someday be reunited in heaven. The tipi always faces east, but every direction has its own special meaning for the tribe.

Dan and his helpers swept the ground clean inside and outside the tipi before the meeting began. They cut enough wood to last through the night and keep the fire burning. The fire must never go out during the ceremony. The inside of the tipi smelled of juniper, which was brought in to burn on the fire to make some aromatic smoke. That is for healing any sickness. Sometimes sage is used to make good smoke.

The chief fanned the fire with his ceremonial fan made of magpie feathers, like the Washoe used in the old days. Feathers have special powers, depending on the bird they came from, but eagle feathers are the most potent. The magpie feathers, darker than the deepest waters of the lake, shimmered in the firelight. The old Washoe often used the feathers from those birds because they're tough and aggressive. They chase predators away from their nests and fearlessly protect what's theirs. That's why warriors liked to put a lone magpie feather in their hair before they went to war.

When everything was ready, Chief Dan said a prayer for the meeting, and we all followed him into the tipi. He sat on the west side of the tipi, and the rest of us went around on the left side and took a seat. The men sat up front near the fire. Women and new members sat at the back, as is the tribal custom, which sometimes rankled this old women's libber, but I deferred to tribal custom. Dan was flanked by the drummer on his right and the cedar helper on his left. The fire keeper sat beside the door of the tipi so he could get more wood when it was needed. Sonseah was our water girl tonight, in place of Dan's wife, who usually carried the water. Her job was to bring cleansing water in at midnight and some food at daybreak, so she had to be at the ready to do her part when the time came. It was an important job that made Sonseah feel important, as she was accustomed to whenever the occasion arose. But all was good tonight. I didn't feel jealous of her as I usually did. She had shown me a softer, kinder side to her personality. Though I didn't know if we would ever really be good friends, we were on the same team and had roles to play for the good of all. It was important that everyone be in a positive frame of mind and that the rules be followed during the meeting so that we could focus on praying and the real reason for this meeting, my daughter's healing.

The drumming and singing began, low and slow at first, like the true Washoe way. My heart beat in steady rhythm with the music. It was good being among my own kind and practicing our ways for the good of those present in the circle, especially Nona. I spent too much time in the White Man's world. I needed this connection with my own people sometimes to remind me who I really am.

The drum had been assembled especially for this meeting with newly washed skin, cinched up so it would stay together and make the best tone. Even the rhythm of Cruiser's and Calamity's tails I'd heard drumming in unison on the pine floor of my cabin was never as soothing to me as the sound of the drummer's steady beating.

Chapter 27

"What is this?" Nona asked.

"It's a special kind of herbal tea. Drink up."

Nona sniffed the liquid, took a sip, and made a face. "Eww, if this is tea, it sure isn't Earl Grey. It tastes terrible."

Nona was right. It wasn't Earl Grey, and this wasn't any tea party. "It's part of the ceremony, Nona. You have to take some of the medicine for it to work its magic. Try to drink a little more, if you can."

Nona steeled herself and took a few more sips of the bitter tea. Then she passed the bowl to me, and I did the same, though I managed to swallow more of it than she did. Everyone in the circle did the same.

Dan beat the drum and sang his songs along with the other men. Each used his own special drumstick to get a different tone. One of the men played a whistle carved from the leg bone of an elk. The music of their voices blending with the rhythmic drumbeats, rattles, and whistles filled every part of the tipi, drifting out into the night and reaching everyone in the whole world. It was like an electrical conduit connecting all our people everywhere. I had my own gourd that my grandfather used, which was passed down to his only child, my mother, after he died. She had still believed like the old Washoe, though, and didn't want to keep anything that belonged to the dead because she thought an angry spirit might be trapped inside it. But the instrument was too old and fine to simply cast aside. To me it was a part of Grandfather, so I changed the rocks and beads inside the gourd and adorned it with my own special feathers from mountain birds to make it mine alone. I played it at every meeting, rattling it gently in rhythm with the thundering drums, and the sound was like hearing rain on the lake in a storm.

The moon rose high above the mountains to illuminate the forest floor, as it had for many generations of my ancestors, but the only light we saw inside the tipi was from the flames of the fire. Dan's drumming never wavered throughout the night, and the songs rose up high and strong like an eagle soaring on great wings spread above the deep blue lake. As I gazed into the fire, I saw figures dancing in the flames keeping time with the drumbeats. Then I beheld images of my mother and my grandfather, who had joined our circle. They seemed so real, I felt as though I could reach out and touch them. I felt the gentle caress of my mother's hand upon my cheek.

Grandfather's pipe smoke rose toward the apex of the tipi and the smoke morphed into the shapes of a bear, eagle, and coyote. Then the smoke transformed into a rainbow of brilliant colors. I could not describe these colors to you because I have never seen anything like them before in nature. Soon I felt something rising up in me along with the white curls of smoke. I had become the smoke.

I had left my body. From high above, I could see Nona inside the tipi and all the other people gathered there in the meeting. Higher and higher I flew until I could see Lake Tahoe from shore to shore and the surrounding Sierra mountain range for many miles. I heard the sounds of thunder rolling across the heavens as I was carried upward on eagle wings through a great wall of white clouds into the blackness of the night.

Traveling higher still, I saw California, the

entire North American continent, the blue marble of Mother Earth, onward beyond the moon and even the Milky Way. Floating, sailing into another realm, I was far beyond the rainbow now, in the spirit world, traveling on a road illuminated by countless stars, to I knew not where. From a distance, I could hear the sound of howling, but it was not the howling of a coyote or a wolf. It was a hound baying.

I didn't know where I was, but I understood it was not a place I had ever been before. I certainly wasn't at Lakeside Shelter, but from all the dogs and other animals I saw, it could have been, except for the fact that this place was beautiful and peaceful, unlike anywhere else I had ever been before. Ahead I saw a bridge of a thousand different colors. The colors vibrated, and a sound like a choir of angels emanated from beyond the bridge. I approached, but I understood that I must not cross over this brilliant span of many colors. Not yet. Though I could see what lay beyond the bridge.

Before me lay a miraculous Eden of endless fields drenched in glorious golden sunshine. The light was almost too bright to look at, but before long my weak human eyes could see clearly into another realm most believe does not exist. Now I knew without any doubt that it did.

Running through endless green pastures, cavorting on the gentle leas, frolicking among sibilant grasses were dogs of every breed, size, and color. Like stars in the heavens, there were so many it was impossible to count them all. Every animal appeared young, happy, and healthy. Among their numbers I saw Dusty and Sandy, my grandparents' mongrel dogs I knew when I was a child. I always loved coming to visit them because I couldn't have dogs in the big city where I lived. I'd spend every summer playing with Dusty and Sandy, and I credit them with my enduring love for dogs. Both dogs were now playful youngsters again, not old and arthritic with grizzled muzzles like the last time I saw them.

I ventured partway across the magical bridge, stopping at its crest so that I could better see what miracles lay beyond. I gazed upon the idyllic scene before me, feeling more at peace than I ever had in my life. At that moment, a basset hound waddled out from among the other dogs and approached the end of the bridge. That explained the distinctive howling I had heard before. The dog was a beautiful white color, like the perfect clouds tumbling above the scene beyond the bridge where I stood. She had the longest snow-white ears with distinctive flecks of gold on their tips. I instantly recognized her from the photos that had appeared in the *Tattler.* This was the ill-fated Gilda.

I summoned Gilda to me. True to her nature, she did not respond to my command to come. Apparently, bassets in the afterlife are as stubborn as Cruiser and Calamity. That is their true hound essence, after all, but of course she didn't know me. I was not her mistress. I tried calling her again, but she only lifted her muzzle to a tangerine sky and bayed mournfully. It was the saddest sound I had ever heard. She was here in a safe, happy place, but her world was still incomplete. I was not the person upon whose arrival she awaited. She waited here for Bertie, not me. Yet I understood that she had summoned me to travel on this incredible journey for some special purpose. I knew I had not been transported all this way for no good reason. Gilda had brought an important message for the one she left behind so tragically and prematurely, and I was chosen to be her courier.

I walked back to my side of the bridge. It was time to return to my earthbound plane. When I turned to look back at beautiful Gilda one last time, she was no longer there.

She had waddled off to join her new pack mates. Joining in a basset chorus, Gilda and the other young hounds scampered down a flower-strewn path of a million delightful scents a heavenly hound like her could track with basset tenacity.

In less than a single beat of a hummingbird's wing, I was back beside Nona inside the tipi. When I saw the light streaming in the doorway of our native tent, I thought at first I was still at Rainbow Bridge, so incredibly brilliant was the light, but I realized it was only the breaking dawn. I was back in my earthbound plane. The drumming had stopped, and the meeting was over.

Sonseah brought a traditional breakfast of fish, pine nut soup, and acorn biscuits and blessed it before we partook. The sunlight was bright, but not as bright as that I had seen on my unforgettable vision during my night journey. I glanced at Nona. She had never appeared so serene to me. She seemed to be glowing from within, and there was an expression of peace and contentment I had never seen before on my daughter's beautiful face. I hadn't felt this close to my only child since the day I held my tiny papoose in my arms for the first time. I hugged her, and hand-in-hand we left the meeting of our Native American Church, feeling more purified than if we'd been baptized a hundred times in the White Man's church. Our peace of mind and spirit wasn't destined to last long, though.

CHAPTER 28

When we stepped out into the new day, we also stepped right into a pack of trouble. Blinding bright lights of another kind were flashing in our eyes, but they were those spinning atop the patrol cars. The law lay in wait for our meeting to adjourn, ready to pounce upon us the moment we exited the tipi. It looked like the whole Tahoe police force was on the scene and ready for a showdown. At least they'd demonstrated enough respect for our tribal customs not to break in on the ceremony before it was over.

"My goodness. All this fuss just for drinking a little herbal tea?"

"Why are the police here, Mom?"

"I think we're about to find out, Nona."

Rusty Cannon approached us, her weapon drawn. Two other officers flanked her.

Who did she think she was, anyway, Annie Oakley? Was she planning to stage her own Wild West Show right here with the tribe outside our tipi? She must have spotted Dan Silvernail's Bowie knife he always carries with him, and that was reason enough for her to cock her six-shooter. This pin-up girl turned policewoman was apparently hell-bent on making her mark in the force, and she was planning on doing it at our expense.

"Put down your weapon," Rusty ordered Dan. He complied.

"What's the trouble, officers?" I asked.

"We're here to take you into custody."

"All of us?" Dan said. "What for?"

"For using an illegal substance."

"We Washoe use our medicine for religious and healing ceremonies. That's what we were doing here. You have no business messing with our religious practices."

"Doesn't matter. It's against the law."

"Do you also arrest Catholics for drinking wine in communion at church?"

"That's not the same thing."

"It is to us, and the cops around here understand that. They don't interfere with our tribal meetings or religion, and you should have been aware of that before the troops were called out on us. You are the one who is breaking the law of the Washoe people."

"Well, let's leave that to the court to decide," Rusty insisted. "All right, officers. Do your duty!"

Rusty and her boys began cuffing everyone who'd attended the meeting, including Nona and me.

We were herded into our rides to the county jail. Nona and I shared the back seat of a cruiser. When I glanced over at her, I saw a tear trail down her cheek. This healing ceremony certainly hadn't turned out as I had hoped it would. Being booked and thrown into the jail was yet more stress my daughter didn't need in her current state. I was worried about her and also about Cruiser and Calamity, who'd been left all alone at my cabin. No one knew how long we would be gone, and I hadn't left any food out for the dogs to eat while we were away. This was one time I wouldn't mind if Calamity raided the pantry. At least she and Cruiser would have something to eat while Nona and I were sharing a cell in our own version of Lakeside Animal Shelter.

This day certainly hadn't ended up as I'd planned. I sure hadn't expected to be peering through the wrong side of the bars of a cell at the county jail when I took Nona along to one of our tribal meetings for a healing ceremony. Thanks to Skip's over-zealous new deputy, half the Washoe tribe had been rounded up and thrown in the clink, including our water girl, Sonseah, who had not taken their interference in native affairs lightly. I rightly guessed that Tahoe law enforcement had not heard the last of this from her. She wasn't one to take such affronts to our tribal traditions lying down.

In fact, when one of the officers tried to put another kind of silver bracelets on her wrists, she didn't hesitate to pick up the ceremonial water bucket and upend it over his head, which he didn't take lightly, either. He completely lost it, but when he started getting a little rough with his dunker, Chief Dan stepped in front of her to block his assault. The officer, who was no peewee himself, surveyed from toes to nose the towering Dan, who tops six foot four, not including his Stetson hat. The cop backed off and decided to continue his cuffing with someone less intimidating.

Sonseah had taken part in lots of demonstrations of one kind or another, which was bound to cause a person to run afoul of the law now and then. She was always protesting about some social issue, particularly if it had anything to do with Washoe affairs, as in the case of Cave Rock. I would gladly pound the pavement for Native American affairs too, but it was mainly anything associated with animal welfare that was sure to get me on the warpath.

However, this was the first time either of us had ended up behind bars for walking a different trail than others did. It appeared that we might be in here for a while. I was getting more concerned by the minute about Cruiser and Calamity. I should have hired a dog sitter or told someone, anyone, where Nona and I were going. Someone had evidently learned about the meeting that was planned last night, or we wouldn't be in our current predicament.

Looking out through the cold steel bars, I finally understood exactly how the animal inmates at the shelter must feel, waiting and waiting for liberation that too often never came. This was the same thing dogs must feel every single time a person walked past their cage at the shelter. I had seen it too often when I toured animal shelters. The hopeful, searching canine eyes looking up whenever someone entered the kennel. *Is it you? Have you come to take me home, at last?* Those eyes always say the same thing, but the answer to their unspoken query is usually the same. Soon, unflagging hope is followed by disappointment and eventually despair when the person they long for never arrives.

Fortunately for us, our freedom was to be quickly restored. When I saw Skip coming down the corridor toward our cell, a flood of relief washed over me as palpably as the contents of Sonseah's upended water bucket had washed over that surprised deputy.

"Beanie, I never expected to see you and Nona in here."

"Neither did we, but here we are, thanks to Deputy Cannon. She's the one responsible for this travesty."

"I already had a talk with her about it. She admitted she was being a little overzealous in executing her duties. You're both free to go."

"Hooray!" Nona said. "Let's blow this joint!'

"What about the rest of us?" Sonseah demanded.

"You, too."

"Thanks, Skip. I owe you one."

"Forget it. If you'd only given me a heads-up about your little tea party, I'd have made sure Rusty had something else to keep her busy for the night. She's new blood, so she doesn't know about all the tribal stuff around Tahoe. I'll see it doesn't happen again."

"Let's hope so," Sonseah piped in.

Dan slipped his big blade into its sheath and strode out of the jail. The rest of the tribe trailed behind him, including my daughter and me. This was one trail of tears we both hoped never to travel again.

CHAPTER 29

The sun dipped low on the western ridge by the time we finally headed for home. A gusting evening wind had come up, and the tips of the pines that surround my property swept the blushing sky like an artist's paintbrush.

For a second time I thought I heard the distant sound of hounds baying, but I discovered it was coming from inside my own house. Nona and I heard the commotion as we pulled into the driveway. Calamity's hysterical yelps drowned out Cruiser's melodious howls.

"That crazy Calamity!" I said. "Who will ever adopt a dog like her with such severe separation anxiety?"

"She seemed all right when we left. Maybe something is wrong with her."

"Something's wrong with her, all right. The dog's a total nut job. I'll never be able to re-home her, and I'll be stuck with her forever. It's no wonder she was dumped at the shelter."

"Gosh, Mom. Cut the poor girl a little slack. We've been gone all night and most of the day."

"True. We've never left her alone so long before, but I assumed that Cruiser's presence would be enough to keep her from going berserk while we were away. I may have to resort to drugging her next time we have to leave her for any period of time. I have some of her remedy on hand from when I first brought her home from the shelter. I should have dosed her with it last night before we left."

As we neared the front door and I heard Cruiser's familiar alarm, I instinctively knew that something more than our long absence had upset the dogs. Calamity was absolved for her bad behavior, at least this time.

"What on earth has gotten into those dogs?" Nona said as we approached the front door.

"I don't know, but something's amiss or Cruiser wouldn't be carrying on so." I knew every subtle nuance of Cruiser's vocalizations and immediately understood that this was certainly no case of separation anxiety on Calamity's part. She was joining in on helping Cruiser guard the home front in our absence. Perhaps she was a better watchdog than I gave her credit for. What were they protecting the house from, though?

When I aimed my key for the lock, I felt the hairs on my neck bristle like the ruff of Cruiser's neck when he spots a cat. It was obvious that someone had tried to break in while we were gone. The door was still shut; only the lock had been damaged. Had the dogs frightened the intruder away, or was he hiding inside the house, waiting to ambush the owner? If that wasn't the case, why were they raising such a ruckus? This wasn't a "Happy to see you; where have you been so long?" greeting.

"You wait out here, Nona."

"Do you think you should go in there alone? What if a burglar is still in the house?"

She was right. It was always wiser to call the police in the case of a break-in, but at the moment, I was more concerned about the dogs' safety than I was my own. Besides, with budget cutbacks and layoffs in the ranks of law enforcement, who knew how long I'd be standing out there waiting for an officer to arrive? Of course, they still had plenty of manpower (and womanpower) to arrest the whole Washoe tribe. This wouldn't be the first crime I'd been first on the scene to investigate.

"Don't worry, I'll be careful. Why don't you see if you can contact Skip on your cell while I check things out?"

"Please be careful, Mom. Here, take my pepper spray with you, just in case. If you see anyone in there, give 'em a shot right in the kisser."

"Gotcha, Dead-eye." There were times like this when I wondered if packing heat might not be a good idea, but pepper spray was about as hot as it was going to get for now.

I nudged the front door open a couple of inches and cringed when the door hinges squealed like a trapped mouse. So much for stealth. I needed a canister of WD40 to go with my pepper spray. The howling basset chorus abruptly ceased, and a black nose popped out the aperture to sniff the air. When Cruiser caught my scent, he whined softly. Immediately, another nose shoved its way through the open door. When Calamity recognized not only my scent but Nona's, she began barking in her usual frenzied manner. I tried shushing her, to no avail. She didn't stop barking until Nona followed me inside.

"I thought I told you to wait outside."

"Sorry. I couldn't stand idly by when you

might be in mortal danger. I figured if there was going to be any trouble, two of us are better than one."

Nona had a valid point. It was the same with bassets. A brace of hounds tracks prey more efficiently than a single dog. Apparently, this twosome trait had worked for Cruiser and Calamity. The thing about bassets is that they have a great big bark to match that big dog's body on short legs. They might be funny-looking to most people, but a formidable voice belies their clownish demeanor. Hearing a basset barking inside a house without actually seeing who's doing the barking, an intruder would assume the dog is much larger than it really is. If a burglar heard two bassets barking in unison, he would no doubt be "braced" for trouble, even though he'd probably only get a good licking if he dared to enter the premises. That was, if he didn't die laughing at the sight of those two silly hound dogs.

Chapter 30

Nona and I relaxed a bit when everything appeared to be in order upon entering the house. Nothing seemed out of place other than the overturned garbage can in the kitchen and the shoe Calamity had been gnawing on. Compared to what we could have found upon our arrival, a chewed loafer seemed inconsequential. Nothing had been stolen. The coast seemed clear.

"Evidently, the dogs scared our would-be thief away before he could enter the house," Nona said.

"It certainly looks that way. He managed to break the door lock, but the noise he made doing that interrupted Cruiser's and Calamity's beauty sleep and put them on high alert. Their barking must have scared him away."

At least that's what I thought until I discovered the back door swinging open and shut in the breeze. Apparently this break-in wasn't an open and shut case, though. The hounds had scared someone off, all right, but whoever it was had been inside the house, awaiting my return. Perhaps we had averted an ambush, after all. So much for the two attack bassets on duty. I could only conclude they'd been bribed with treats to gain entry into their territory. Hand over a few Snausages or Bacon Beggin' Strips and these fearsome watchdogs would probably roll out the Welcome Home Invaders mat. Either that, or the interloper was someone they recognized.

Rusty Cannon strode from Skip's patrol car, ready to add more notches to her Sam Browne with another arrest. Not Nona and me again, I hoped. I'd seen as much as I ever cared to see of the El Dorado County jail.

"What are *you* doing here?" I said. "We were expecting Sheriff Cassidy."

"He couldn't respond to a burglary. He has bigger fish to fry."

Officer Shapely must have known fisherman Skip a lot better than I first thought she did. Just how well, I didn't know. Maybe the Skipper had even taken her out in his new speedboat for a moonlight cruise. I was merely the first mate on the good ship *Trout Scout.*

"What seems to be the problem?"

"Someone broke into my house."

Rusty immediately spotted the jimmied lock on the front door. "So I see. Did you go inside before calling us?"

"Yes."

"You should have waited for the police to arrive, ma'am."

Smile when you say that, Sister. Words like that used to grind my gears, but as I grow older, I am beginning to find *ma'am* preferable to *sweetie, honey,* or *dear.* Worst of all is *young lady,* especially if being delivered by a young man in the guise of courtesy.

Of course, I imagine women like Rusty have their own special crosses to bear. It seems that no matter what a woman's age, respect is something we must constantly fight hard to earn in our society, and I guessed that was what Rusty was all about. She was fighting to gain respect in her profession and earn a decent living, all the while bumping her head on the ceiling that was still impenetrable for all but the most ambitious females. While you might expect Rusty's good looks to work in her favor, they could turn out to be her Waterloo with the sheriff's office, especially now that she'd been officially outed as a centerfold.

"That might have been too long. Besides, whoever was here is gone now, Officer. He probably broke in while my daughter and I were locked up in jail." I hoped my intended sarcasm wasn't lost on her, but if it wasn't, she probably didn't care. In her estimation, she had just been doing her duty when she set up the ambush at our prayer meeting. If there was one thing positive you could say about Officer Cannon, it was that she was tenacious in the execution of her duties. Once on the trail, you couldn't distract her from her quarry for anything. In fact, if she were a dog, she'd be a basset hound.

Even though I'd said the intruder was gone, Rusty followed standard procedure, just in case I was wrong about that assumption. It was decidedly preferable to have Officer Rusty on your side than not.

"You both had better wait out here while I take a look inside, just to be sure it's all clear."

"Cruiser! Calamity!" I didn't want the dogs to get caught in the crossfire, in case there was about to be a shootout at the OK-9 Corral. Cruiser responded right away, but no Calamity appeared, even when I summoned her again. Nothing unusual about that.

For the second time that day, Rusty drew her weapon. She entered my home cautiously, making her way slowly but steadily through each room. I heard her yelling "Clear!" as she finished scanning each room of my house for a possible burglary suspect. I guessed she was following that procedure mostly to assure herself, since no other officers were present who would have needed to know the coast was clear.

Everything was going fine until she made her way into my kitchen, the last room on her search. Then, I heard Rusty shout out the command, "Freeze!" Had she found someone hiding in the house after all? How could I have missed that? I'm not exactly an amateur when it comes to sniffing out criminals, but I'm sure no pistol-packin' momma. For the first time since I'd met her, I was glad that Officer Cannon was on the scene and ready for action. When I heard a single shot fired inside the house, I couldn't wait out on the front porch any longer. I charged in the door, with Nona and Cruiser close behind, despite my insistence that they stay out. I couldn't argue with Nona right now. Officer Cannon could be in trouble. And where was that naughty Calamity?

"Is everything all right, Officer?"

"Yes."

From the bullet hole in my kitchen ceiling, I wasn't so sure.

"If everything's all right, what were you firing at?"

"I almost shot your dog!"

Frantic, Nona cried out. "Calamity! Calamity! Where are you?"

A nose popped out of the pantry and sniffed the traces of Cannon shot in the air.

Nona coaxed the frightened dog. "Come on out, girl. It's okay."

"What happened?"

"I was just checking to make sure no one was hiding in your pantry. I must have surprised her. She leapt out at me. I thought I was being attacked and fired off a round. I wasn't expecting to be ambushed by a hound dog."

One ambush deserves another, Officer Nasty. "I guess she wasn't expecting you, either. She was probably already spooked by the intruder."

Of course, Nona and I knew that the pantry was where you'd usually find Calamity, but she was hiding there now for good reason. She was afraid of thunder, so the sound of gunfire at close range should have sent her right through the roof along with that stray bullet. I was just glad the rookie's aim was off and that no harm had been done. At least that's what I thought until I noticed the drops of blood staining the linoleum on my kitchen floor.

"Whose blood is this on the floor? Are you sure you didn't shoot the dog?" I said, suddenly concerned about Calamity. Perhaps she was hurt, and that's why she had been hiding in the pantry. She might have been injured by the intruder and that's why she reacted as she did to the officer when she opened the pantry door.

Nona examined Calamity from the tip of her nose to the last hair on her tail for any wound. "There's no mark on her. She isn't hurt, Mom."

Well, that was welcome news in more than one way. No more vet visits were in our immediate future.

"Did Calamity bite you, Officer?"

"No, although I wouldn't have taken any bets on it when she came hurtling out of there at me. She meant business. She was growling and seemed very aggressive, which is why I fired off a shot."

"We've had some behavioral issues with her since I rescued her from Lakeside Shelter, and I saw some fear aggression from her at a shelter worker, but she has never bitten anyone that I know of."

"So far, you mean."

"To be perfectly honest with you, I wouldn't take any bets on that, either. I'm glad she didn't bite you, though." Was I ever! I didn't need this gal to file a lawsuit against me too, like she was threatening to do to the whole sheriff's office.

"Perhaps it was the uniform she's wearing, Mom. Lots of dogs don't like them. You know how dogs react to postal carriers."

Yep, Calamity definitely didn't like uniforms, or veterinary lab coats, either. I remembered how she had reacted to Rex at the shelter whenever he approached her. He wore a uniform, too. This could have been no more than a post-traumatic shelter disorder flashback for Calamity. Or could it have been Rex who had paid us a visit and bled on my kitchen floor after Calamity finally gave him a well-deserved retaliatory bite?

Sleep eluded me that night, but it had nothing to do with my occasional insomnia episodes. Pine branches clawed the outer cabin walls in the windstorm that had increased to gale force. Rain pelted the roof in a relentless downpour. Every time I heard the house creaking against the storm's power, my neck hair spiked. Was it only the storm, or had our intruder returned?

We'd managed to blockade the front door since the lock was broken, but once your home has been invaded, you never feel truly safe again. Having a home alarm system of two barking dogs helped make me feel a bit more secure, but the knowledge that the hounds were here wasn't putting me at ease tonight, especially with Cruiser snoring away at the foot of the bed, drooling blissfully on his quilt. It was hard to stretch out enough to relax with a seventy-pound hound taking up half the bed. His presence was always a comfort, though. Still, I suspected that if Jack the Ripper were lurking outside my bedroom door, Cruiser would never be the wiser. That dog could really count his Zs.

As for me, counting sheep, or bassets, has never worked to induce slumber. It's hard to quiet my mind at times like this, so the only thing that helps me is to do a little novel plotting in my head until I finally drift off. That worked fine under normal circumstances, but right now all I could think of was who might have had a reason to break into my home and what that reason could be.

Instead of the usual cast of literary characters, a list of possible suspects roiled in my brain like the black storm clouds blustering their way over the peaks of majestic Mount Tallac. I doubt even Charles Dickens himself could have imagined the likes of Victoria Thatcher for a character in one of his novels. But people in Dickens's day never wore their hair dyed purple, and the only multiple piercings, chains, or spikes were to be found deep in the dungeons of the Tower of London's bloody history.

I had such a painful assortment of body aches from the physical and emotional strain of this case, not to mention chasing that crazy Calamity from one end of Lake Tahoe to the other, I felt like I was being pierced and poked with spikes. As though thoughts of Tori weren't enough to chase the Sandman away and hit him on the head with his own sandbags, there was always the executioner, Rex, who was probably the scariest-looking fellow I'd seen inside or outside an animal shelter. Now there was a bedtime bogeyman that could make anyone want to pull the covers over her head or hide under the bed. His sheer size was enough to make me suspect he could easily have killed Rhoda. I already knew he was certainly capable of efficiently administering death to any living thing, but whether meting out a death sentence at the shelter also included his boss, I still didn't know. It seemed as if he had more in common with her temperamentally than anyone else I'd yet encountered while investigating this case, so what would be his motive to kill her? Perhaps he just detested her as much as every other employee at Lakeside and every pet lover in Tahoe did.

There was also Bertie Finch, whose dear Gilda had tragically died at Rhoda's command. Perhaps of all the possible motives for Rhoda's death, I could understand Bertie's the best. I know if it were Cruiser instead of Gilda, and I had been in Bertie's shoes, that would be more than enough motive to make Rhoda suffer the same fate.

I still had a large collection of possible suspects to consider as the perpetrator of Rhoda's killing. From what I'd heard about the victim and seen of her myself when visiting the shelter, I could easily understand why she was so vehemently disliked by all who knew her. As Sally had said when asked who would want Rhoda Marx dead, her answer was the same as mine. Who wouldn't?

Chapter 31

Nona was up long before me, which was unusual. I'm normally an early riser, but even Cruiser was up before me that morning. The same thing lured me as lured him from the comfort of the bed — the smell of food. I could never resist the aroma of warm cinnamon buns. Like a hungry hound, I tracked the scent and found the hot buns and also Cruiser. He was exactly where I would expect to find him hanging out, in the kitchen. He and Calamity flanked Nona at the dinette table, waiting for handouts or accidental droppage.

"Hey, lazybones. You're finally up. Even Cruiser was awake before you today."

"I had trouble getting to sleep last night. I didn't even feel him get off the bed. I guess I was out cold."

"Did the storm keep you awake, too?"

"That and worrying about what happened last night."

"It's enough to make you worry. You keep putting yourself and Cruiser at risk, getting involved in all these crazy cases up here. When are you going to retire and enjoy life a little?"

"I'm only fifty. That's not exactly retirement age. Fifty is the new forty, haven't you heard? Besides, I do enjoy my life."

"You know what I mean. I wish you'd do something that doesn't involve putting yourself in danger all the time. Like your writing."

"When I become a rich and famous author, I can rest on my laurels, or on my front porch knitting Afghans."

"With you, that would be Afghan hounds, wouldn't it, Mom?"

"Hounds of some kind or other, I suppose."

Nona knew I craved the excitement of crime-solving, but sometimes it got a little too exciting, even for me. When danger crawled right up on my front porch and invaded my inner sanctum, that was cause for real alarm, so I understood her concern. I knew she was looking out for me — and my best buddy, of course.

"Do you have any ideas about who our intruder might have been?"

"I was counting possibilities like sheep last

night, which is why I didn't get much sleep."

"I had a little trouble myself with all that rain pounding on the roof."

"I know. You'd have thought we did a rain dance last night in the tipi."

"What exactly did we do last night in the tipi, Mom?"

"It was a healing ceremony, in the true Washoe tradition."

"Have you told Skip about it?"

"No. He's my best friend, but he's as white as Wonder Bread and doesn't really understand the ways of our people. It's better for us both if it stays that way."

"I think you're probably right. That whole experience was pretty intense, but I'm glad you took me there with you."

"Me, too."

"Did you ever get hold of Skip?"

"No. I left a message on his phone, but he hasn't gotten back to me yet."

"You really should report the break-in. Others in the community might be in jeopardy."

"You're right, honey. I think I'll go over after I finish my breakfast and pay the sheriff a little visit."

Nona was right that any crime should be reported, but I had the uncomfortable feeling that I was the only one who should be worried about more trouble.

It was nearing ten A.M. by the time I drove over to Skip's place. His patrol car was still parked in the driveway, which seemed unusual, considering it wasn't his day off and there were crimes that needed solving; namely, the Marx murder and now a home invasion. Had he taken the day off sick? That could explain why he hadn't responded to my message.

I rang the bell. No response. I knocked once. Twice. Finally, I heard the sound of footsteps. The door opened to reveal a disheveled Skip still cloaked in his bathrobe. Skip's skinny legs reminded me of those on the seagulls I used to see hanging around Fisherman's Wharf. His hair looked like a haystack on his head, and sprigs of straw-colored chest hair poking out the top of his robe made me think this scarecrow needed re-stuffing.

"Beanie, what are you doing here?"

"You haven't answered any of my phone messages. I thought something might be wrong, so I came over to check on you. Are you sick or something?"

"Uh, er, yeah. Something."

"You took the day off?"

"Yes, I did. Do I need a doctor's note?"

"No, of course not." Where was this defensive attitude coming from? My question was quickly answered when I heard a female voice beckon from inside.

"Who's that, Skippy?"

I'd heard that voice somewhere before, but it wasn't the nasal twang of Rita Ramirez.

"I can't talk now. I'll give you a call later, okay?"

"Sure. Okay. Later."

The door clicked shut. I didn't need a farmhouse to drop on me to deduce what was going on. Skip was taking the day off, but it wasn't because he was sick. Far from it. Skippy got lucky. If his hair looked like hay, it was because he'd had a roll in it. I didn't have to be Sherlock Holmes to figure out who his lucky charm was.

As I drove away, puzzling over Skip's odd behavior, I realized I forgot why I had come over to talk to him in the first place. I didn't even get a chance to tell him about the intruder at my house last night. Apparently, if any sleuthing was to be done on this crime, it would be up to me and my only witnesses — the drooling duo, Cruiser and Calamity.

I was dying to share this juicy tidbit about Skip with Nona, but I didn't want to gossip about my friend behind his back. I had the feeling that news of this collaboration was going to make the rounds in the community and his department without any help from me, like a "Cannon" shot heard 'round the lake.

Chapter 32

I made sure I was the first person on the scene at the town hall meeting. I intended to make sure I had the best vantage point and would have a basset's-eye view of every attendee — that would be from the knees up, of course. I would observe everyone as intently as Calamity and Cruiser watch my every movement in the kitchen and around the house. In the same way they patiently await the incidental dropping of any tidbit that might fall within easy reach, I would be watching everyone's actions for any suspicious behavior and listening for revealing statements that might incriminate a killer who could be lurking among the crowd. I had brought my mini tape recorder along with me to record the meeting secretly from within my shirt pocket, so I didn't have to rely much on my memory, which seemed to fail me every now and then.

While I had aced Mr. Walker's typing class

in high school, I found shorthand in Mr. Dudley's class a far more difficult subject to learn. All those odd squiggles and swirls looked like Egyptian hieroglyphs to me. I never knew what any of them meant, and I got a D in Dudley's class to prove it. Besides typing, my best class was English. The fact that I had a crush on handsome Mr. Curran, who had a thick Welsh accent and large hairy hands, didn't hurt. Whenever he helped me with an essay and his furry arm accidentally brushed against mine, I had to stifle a giggle because it tickled me like fuzz on a caterpillar. I was always getting crushes on my teachers, most recently Professor Blayne, which ended rather disastrously. But I never had a crush on Mr. Dudley, mainly because he could crush any student in his class. He must have weighed at least 500 pounds. His car was fitted with a special steering wheel that adjusted so he could get into it.

Too bad about the shorthand; fortunately, some genius invented tape recorders for people like me, so as it turns out, I didn't need to know shorthand after all. Nyah, nyah, Mr. Fuddy Duddy Dudley. Using my mini-tape, I was free to focus more on observing the goings-on at the meeting than trying to scribble every word down on paper. I could also refer to the tape for reference material when it came time to write my article. Nothing like a taped conversation for assuring the accuracy of quotations.

However, I find it's not always what people say but how they say it that reveals their true nature and underlying intentions. Do they blink a lot or avert their eyes from yours whenever they talk? Or do they gaze at you unblinkingly, as some skilled liars can do with the greatest of ease? Does a gesture or barely perceptible facial tic betray a false statement? Body language is truly the universal language. People don't even need have to open their mouths to tell you what you need to know about them. All you had to do was watch George W. Bush blink and smirk his way through a press conference to know he was lying like Barney on the Oval Office rug. Perhaps Barney perceived something about his commander-in-chief that most people couldn't, and that's why he didn't seem to like ol' George very much. Dogs are great judges of character.

I have learned how to observe, but mastering the art of listening is equally important. I don't have an ear for music, but I have two ears for crime-busting, like Cruiser does. Liars betray themselves with their voice inflections and variations in speech cadence, which often speeds up when someone tells a lie. If you listen to the police questioning of Lee Harvey Oswald when he was apprehended after the assassination of President John Kennedy, you know he's not telling the truth. All I had to do was rewind and play my tape over and over as many times as necessary to pick up on anything I might have missed the first time around. If only life worked the same way. There are certainly one or two things in my life I'd love to rewind, not the least of them the untimely loss of my husband. I suspected that Roberta Finch felt much the same about the loss of her dog, Gilda.

Half an hour before the meeting was scheduled to begin, the room was filled to capacity with people from the community who were either for or against the building of a new shelter. Mostly they were for it, which boded well for our camp, but we had to convince the council members to take a stand for the animals. When it comes to money versus mutts, money usually prevails.

All the Found Hounds volunteers were present, including Bertie Finch and Jenna Fairbanks. Amanda Peabody and other shelter employees were also there, although it wasn't so easy to determine which side of the kennel fence they were on with regard to this issue. Whether they would argue for or against a new shelter seemed to hinge on budgetary concerns. Even if they got their new shelter, they had to be able to sustain its operation, and the money for that had to come from someplace. While most of the employees cared just as much about animal welfare as Found Hounds or TAILS did, no one wanted to sacrifice his or her job in the bargain. Paychecks are too hard to come by these days.

I might have guessed that the last one to arrive at the meeting would be none other than the Princess of Piercings, Tori Thatcher. Her late entrance was no doubt staged for maximum drama. She wanted everyone in the community to know that she was a force to be reckoned with in this issue. When Tori entered the room, all heads snapped in her direction, and it wasn't because of her purple spiked hair and tattoos. Maybe the crowd's reaction had a little bit to do with her unusual appearance, but it probably had more to do with the fact that the whole TAILS organization trailed after Tori carrying bold placards protesting the abuses that had gone on for too long at Lakeside Shelter: Lakeside, the Animals' Abu Graib! Shut Down the Pound! I probably wasn't the only one in the room who had the uncomfortable feeling that a demonstration of another type was imminent.

Chapter 33

Members of the city council were doubtlessly hoping for a quick and easy resolution to the shelter quagmire, but by no stretch of the imagination would this be quick and or easy. Tori the Terrible would make certain of that. Her presence at any public gathering was like shaking a bottle of Coca Cola before popping the cap. It was obvious after a few minutes that the lid was about to blow off this meeting over what should be done about Lakeside Shelter. Once the floor was open to public comment, the dogs of dissent were definitely let out.

"Shut down the pound!" Tori blasted like a diesel truck horn. She sure didn't need a microphone to get her message heard. Everyone was a bit taken aback by the sheer volume of her androgynous voice, which matched her demeanor and appearance. But that was nothing compared to the sound of the whole group of demonstrators howling in chorus like so many basset hounds.

"Down with the Pound! Down with the Pound!" If only Cruiser and Calamity had been there, they could have joined in, too. "Roo-roo, Aarooo!"

Only the pounding of a gavel managed to quell the growling of the "down with the pound" pack. Once the room had quieted down, Mayor Thor Petersen spoke up. "I think we are probably all in agreement that the past management of Lakeside Shelter has left much to be desired."

"That's the understatement of the century," Roberta Finch snipped.

"A new manager will take over the operation of the shelter as soon as we've found the best person for the job," the mayor said. "We've already begun to . . ."

Bertie cut Thor off mid-sentence, which annoyed him, but she obviously didn't care. After I had shared with her Gilda's message from beyond Rainbow Bridge, she seemed even more resolute in her intention to see the dismantling of the shelter where Gilda had met her untimely end. "I'm in total agreement that Lakeside Shelter should be shut down for good. No one who loves animals and knows the history of the place would ever want to set foot in it. It's high time Tahoe had a new shelter."

"I think we all would like to see Tahoe have a state-of-the-art shelter, Ms. Finch, but building a new shelter presents some challenges. The first of those, of course, is budgetary. The other is finding adequate space to accommodate a building project of this scope. Undeveloped land that is not National Forest is somewhat limited at Lake Tahoe. I do agree that we need a larger facility to meet the demand, but funding concerns may not make that possible. We're looking, instead, into updating the existing structure to handle more animals."

"Codswallop!" Bertie barked. "You seem to find ample funds for other pet projects in the community that having nothing to do with the welfare of people's pets."

Amanda Peabody piped in. "While you're at it, how about funding a program to educate the public on how to better care for their companion animals? If people were more responsible for their pets' welfare and spayed and neutered their animals, perhaps we wouldn't need a bigger shelter."

"Amanda's right," Jenna Fairbanks said. "What we need is a state-of-the-art spay/neuter clinic with veterinarians on our staff to do the surgeries. A similar facility in Sacramento does ten thousand such surgeries a year! We also need behaviorists and trainers who can rehabilitate adoptable pets. The more of them we can re-home, the fewer need be destroyed. That's a job none of us wants to do . . . well, almost none."

No one had to guess who Jenna was referring to, and my guess was that no one in the room would shed any tears for Rhoda Marx, least of all Tori. She didn't seem the type to shed tears for anyone or anything. What good did tears ever do for the animals' plight, anyway? Even she understood that action is what brings about change in our increasingly complacent, self-centered world. And more often than not, it takes extreme action to occupy the public's attention. If the pen is mightier than the sword, Tori's tongue was mightier still. I had the feeling there was absolutely nothing she and her cohorts wouldn't do to accomplish their goal of raising public awareness about animal welfare. They probably would think nothing of splashing red paint on anyone wearing a fur coat or of marching naked down Lake Tahoe Boulevard to promote their cause. But had they gone as far as committing murder for the animals?

Sometimes it's not who is present but who is not that provides me with a needed clue, and there was one person who was conspicuously absent from this meeting. Conspicuous, because he would be impossible to miss if he were present. The only staff member from the shelter who had not joined the town hall meeting was Rex, the kennel attendant I'd met at Lakeside Shelter. And, of course, Rhoda Marx couldn't make it either because, like the animals entrusted to Rex's care, she was another one to "bite the dust," as he sang when leading the next victim of pet overpopulation down the gray mile. Had Rhoda been forced to walk the mile with Rex, too? She would have had a hard time fending off someone his size.

When Mayor Petersen and the council focused their attention on finding a new shelter manager, I could only hope that Rex's name wasn't on a short list for the position. In my way of thinking, he wouldn't be an improvement over his former boss, Rhoda. Of all the personnel I had met at Lakeside Shelter, he was the only one, besides Rhoda, who really seemed to be "into" his line of work.

I know that animal police and shelter staff try their best to assume an air of detachment as a way of distancing themselves from the emotionally charged environment in which they work daily. It is too easy for most to become attached to the dogs and cats they take into their care, but with Rex you could sense that there was no danger of his becoming attached to any of the animals he attended to. This was clearly only a job to him, and that wasn't the ideal employee to have working at a shelter. Too often with people like him in such a setting abuses can occur, as Calamity's response to Rex suggested might have been the case before she was released from Lakeside into my care. A compassionate heart should be a prerequisite for working with animals in any setting, as anyone who'd had dealings with Lakeside Shelter under "euthanasia expert" Marx's management would agree.

CHAPTER 34

Reporting on the meeting about the shelter would be a challenge. There wasn't much to report because no agreement had been reached about building a new shelter. Regardless of public sentiment, it would be business as usual at Lakeside Shelter, but some changes were implemented to help keep the peace.

Besides putting the shelter under new management, the council made a few concessions to improve pound policy. They decided to update their scanning system to a universal scanner that could detect any brand of chip and made it mandatory for staff to scan all incoming strays for a microchip and make every effort to contact the owner. The holding period was increased from only three days to one week, and longer in the case of more easily adoptable dogs and purebreds, which would improve the odds of survival in the future for dogs like Gilda. They also made it easier for local animal rescue groups to try to re-home adoptable dogs and cats.

The changes helped to quell some, but not all, of the public rancor over the shelter. Animal activists and welfare groups would not be completely satisfied until the outdated Lakeside Shelter was history and a new shelter was constructed to take its place. We had a long way to go before that would become a reality. It became sort of a double-dog dare to do everything in our power to make our dream a reality, and we all vowed to redouble our efforts to raise money and solicit donors for a new shelter. There's a lot of money in Tahoe, if you know where to look for it. Fortunately, there are a lot of animal lovers with money to throw at a worthy cause like a new animal shelter.

The word about our upcoming Bassetille Day event had spread far and wide, thanks to articles and announcements I'd submitted to national pet magazines and newspapers throughout California and beyond. The number of expected attendees was rising so fast, we were going to have to find a venue large enough to accommodate them all. Where else would that be but Alpine Paws Park, Tahoe's new dog park right on the lake? Although the off-leash park might be a bit more crowded with dogs than usual, the increase in the number of attendees was great news for the homeless hounds. We'd be taking in more money, but the best part was that dogs like Calamity stood a better chance of being adopted.

However, she wouldn't find a new home without some basic training, and that was how I ended up at an evening dog training class at Petropolis. Nona had flaked out on me, which surprised me since she seemed so enamored with Calamity. It wasn't because she had a date, which was her usual excuse to me about anything she didn't want to do. She said she had a headache, so I didn't press her. I've had enough cranium crushers myself. Perhaps she'd inherited a tendency for migraines from me. Whatever the reason, I understood that she wanted to be alone.

I left Cruiser behind to comfort Nona. Handling two strong-willed basset hounds at once is a two-person job. Just keeping Calamity from sampling the treats at Petropolis would be daunting. Tonight's training session would be no different.

Getting her in the front door of the pet store was the first challenge. Being in a mall the size of Petropolis was sensory overload for humans, let alone dogs. I feared that this excursion with Calamity wasn't going to go much better than our experience at the vet had.

The whoosh of the electric doors gave her such a fright, she nearly became airborne. Once we were inside the store, she did a kind of canine crab walk down the aisle, hunkering as close to the floor as she possibly could. Pulling me along, she kept peering up at everything and everyone as though she was about to be eaten by some alien life form. The rawhide chews and other yummy treats stored in basset-level bins didn't slow her down one bit. All she wanted was out the nearest exit as quickly as possible. Only when she spotted the other dogs inside the training arena did she appear to relax any. Her stance was more erect, and I even discerned a slight tail wag. Being around my gregarious Cruiser for a while had socialized her some, evidently.

I had less trouble guiding her into the training ring. A young woman wearing a blue coat with a Petropolis logo greeted us. Thank goodness it wasn't a white coat, or Calamity would have thought I was taking her to the vet again.

"Welcome. I'm Trixie. I'll be your trainer tonight. We'll be starting class in a few minutes, so go ahead and find a place over there with the other students." I thought it a bit odd that Trixie didn't even acknowledge her new four-legged student. Did this woman even like dogs? Perhaps she recognized trouble when she saw it. I just hoped that Trixie could teach this dog some new tricks.

I didn't have to find my place. Calamity found one for us right away. She dragged me straight over to where the other owners were trying to keep their dogs in check while waiting impatiently for the training class to begin. At least Calamity was social with the other dogs. She wanted to make friends with all of them. And she hadn't bitten anyone. Yet.

There were the usual assortment of small dogs, mostly terriers, a hyper cocker spaniel, and a couple of large breeds, including a goofy old English sheepdog and another basset hound. When Calamity spotted him, she tried to make friends. He was obviously a show dog, which the owner was quick to point out in case there was any confusion about that on my part.

His owner shifted uncomfortably in her seat when Calamity approached her dog. She wanted to stay as far away as possible from my lowly shelter hound so that Champion Milford of Mandeville Acres would not catch anything from her, including poor breeding and bad manners. The blue-blood basset seemed to have the same haughty attitude as his owner. The basset's demeanor is typically blasé, but even Cruiser hadn't given poor Calamity such a cold shoulder upon their first meeting.

Milford sniffed at her briefly and then scratched at his ear. Perhaps it was an infection brewing inside the ear canal, a constant problem for dogs bred for long ears like his and Calamity's. After Milford finished scratching, he gave a shake of his exceptionally pendulous flews, showering everyone within range in slobber. Believe it or not, show dogs can transform any gathering into a total slobberfest, but not even Cruiser could produce that much spit. Even His Highness Milford didn't pass the first lesson of tonight's training class, along with Calamity. Evidently, Trainer Trixie was not familiar with the rather unique qualities of the basset hound, not the least of them being a stubborn streak a mile wide and twice as long. Getting a basset to do anything on command is a tall order. Treats are a plus to achieve results, but even treats were no help here.

"All right, everyone. Command your dog

to sit." Trixie instructed. Most of the dogs did a perfect sit on command the first time, except for the sheepdog, who would rather have been off herding sheep somewhere, though there aren't any sheep herds in Tahoe. *Sit* is a pretty basic command, and some dogs had obviously already learned it before coming to the class. When a couple of dogs didn't get the idea right off, their owners had to help them learn the command. "Don't push on the dog's rear. Draw his attention to your face, then lift up on his leash," Trixie said. "He'll just naturally sit down."

After a few tries, all the dogs were sitting on command with no problem. Both of the bassets responded to the command too, but instead of squatting on their haunches like the other dogs, they lounged on one hip. That wouldn't pass muster for this trainer.

"No, no!" Trixie said. "That's not a proper sit." She tried every way possible to induce the bassets to lift up their assets and get into a proper sit, as her other students had done.

"You silly woman, that *is* how a basset hound sits," Milford's owner declared.

"It is not a correct sit on command," Trixie insisted.

"She's right, you know." I hated to agree

with Ch. Milford's snooty mistress, but facts were facts. "Basset hounds have a long spine, which makes it impossible for them to sit upright like other breeds do. You'd no doubt have the same problem if one of your students was a dachshund or a corgi."

"Well, I'm afraid it won't do in my class."

"Come along, Milford." Milford's owner led him out of the training ring. He followed behind her as she marched to the manager to insist on a refund. I wanted to show Miss Trixie a few tricks of my own. I would have led Calamity out right behind Milford, but I wasn't about to do anything that would prevent my foster hound from getting the training that might help her find a permanent home. Even if she flunked the class, at least she'd get some much-needed instruction and socialization in the bargain. For this dog, even a little training was better than none at all. She was bound to acquire some improvement in her behavior by osmosis. At least I hoped so, for her sake . . . and mine! One way or another, I was determined to find this dog another home when it came time for the Basset Waddle.

CHAPTER 35

By the time our training class was over, I don't know who was more exhausted from the experience, Calamity or me. I wasn't sure whether to attribute her not tugging at the end of her leash to fatigue or to having actually learned some leash manners in the class. Either way, I was grateful that she wasn't dragging me out of Petropolis. Our exit was certainly an improvement over our entrance. When I put her back in her travel carrier, she instantly curled up and fell asleep. This dog needed training classes every night to wear her out. It worked even better than Doc Heaton's miracle drug.

When we got home, Nona was dozing in Tom's old chair with Cruiser at her side. I don't know how many times I had come home to find Tom doing the same thing. Cruiser stirred from his slumber when he heard us come in. Nona woke up, too. Cruiser got up and came to greet me. He gave Calamity the once-over, reading the various scents on her coat that revealed to him where she'd been all evening. His attentiveness to her made me think he may have missed his crazy little houseguest. Were they starting to bond and become pack mates, despite my best-laid plans?

"Hi, Mom. Back already?"

"What do you mean, already? That was the longest two hours of my life."

"Sorry I couldn't go with you."

"Did your headache get any better?"

"Yes. I took a couple of your pills."

"I'd better take a couple myself. I have a headache now, too."

"How did Calamity do?"

"She learned to sit, heel, and stay. I didn't think she had it in her. I was proud of her."

"What a good girl you are!" Calamity plodded over to Nona and flopped down atop her slippers. I could tell that she was glad to be in familiar territory again, but I knew it was also her way of claiming Nona. I hoped she wasn't going to become too attached before we could find another home for her. It would be hard placing her in yet another unfamiliar environment if she became too comfortable here.

Like any other shelter dog, what this dog needed more than anything was some stability in her life. How can you ever have any kind of normal life when you can never depend on anyone to consistently love and care for you? How can you feel secure while being bounced from shelter to shelter or from home to home? The damage done to the psyche is no different for these sensitive creatures than it is for a human being. Too often the emotional trauma is irreversible.

I also feared it might be just as hard for Nona to let Calamity go. Calamity eased her way onto the ottoman Cruiser-style. I knew I probably shouldn't let her climb up on the furniture, at least until she knew who was top dog in the pack, but I was too tired to make a fuss. Watching Nona stroke the dog's silky soft ears, I knew she was becoming attached to her in spite of herself. But I also knew she couldn't house a dog that size in her high-rise San Francisco apartment. At some level Nona knew it, too. Perhaps that was the real reason she had opted not to take Calamity to her first training class, because she was hesitant to bond any further with a dog she would ultimately have to part with. I suppose that's why there are so many foster flunkies who grow too attached to their fostered fur children and can't part with them. If Calamity wasn't such a problem child, I'm sure I'd end up the same way.

"I think I'm going to turn in."

"So early?"

"I'd love to sit up with you a while, dear, but I'm really beat tonight. You should go to bed, too. You don't want that headache coming back."

"I think I'll sit out here with the dogs and read for a while."

"Good. I can have some time alone in my bed before Cruiser makes his move. Don't stay up too late now."

"I won't. Oh, I almost forgot to tell you that Amanda Peabody from Lakeside Shelter called. She says they've had more trouble down at the shelter."

"Trouble? What kind of trouble? It's not another . . ."

"No, it's nothing like that. She didn't say exactly what, but she asked if you could come over to the shelter tomorrow and see her."

"Okay. Thanks for letting me know." Frankly, I wish Nona had waited until morning to tell me about Amanda's phone call. Quality sleep was hard enough to come by lately. All I needed was something else weighing on my mind for a good nocturnal toss-and-turn session.

I find I sometimes have better luck drifting off to sleep when I am using the creative part of my mind trying to craft an article opening or plot a chapter of a book rather than fretting about a problem, although I have often arrived at solutions to problems in my sleep. Tonight it was thinking about the upcoming Bassetille Day that finally brought the Sand Basset waddling along to sprinkle me with magic drool to help me off to dreamland. The last thing I remember was Cruiser climbing up on his usual spot at the foot of the bed and settling down on his Raining Cats and Dogs quilt for a long night's slumber.

Cruiser and I were at the Basset Waddle. He was winning all the contests with ease. Calamity was there too, running amok and creating havoc at every opportunity. She ran away from me, and I took off running after her, hollering at the top of my lungs. She completely ignored me, of course. Finally, I caught up with her and led her back to where I'd left Cruiser. He was gone! After searching for him everywhere, in desperation I found myself at Lakeside Shelter. The place was deserted, except for all the animals barking, howling, and meowing their lament. I searched every kennel, but Cruiser was nowhere to be found. Desperate, I began to cry. Where was my boy?

Suddenly, I found myself standing in front of Kennel 9. There was a basset hound inside, but it wasn't Cruiser. It was a female basset. At first I thought it must be Calamity, but it wasn't. This dog was a lemon and white variety of the breed, almost a golden color. The light shone on the dog's brass nametag. The name on the tag said Gilda.

All at once, the door to the kennel flew open with a bang that echoed through the shelter. Gilda waddled out. Looking sadder than any basset I'd ever seen (and that's saying a lot), she headed down the gray mile very slowly. She stopped once and turned to look back at me sorrowfully. I understood that she wanted me to follow her, so I did. We came to the door of the euthanasia room. Gilda walked right through it!

I opened the door and followed the phantom dog to the euthanasia chamber. I looked through the viewing panel. Cruiser was inside! I screamed and opened up the chamber. When I opened it, he stood up and walked into my arms. I hugged him with all my might, but he pulled away and followed Gilda through the door. I realized that Cruiser was dead.

Next thing I knew I was the one trapped inside the chamber, which was filling with deadly gas. I gasped for air. My life was slipping away as I felt a sensation of being smothered slowly, slowly . . .

Gasping for breath, I yanked the pillow from off my head. Cruiser had apparently nudged my down-filled pillow onto my face when he wormed his way up to the head of the bed. I had probably been thrashing around so much in my nightmare that even he couldn't sleep. I didn't make him resume his place at the foot of the bed but let him snuggle under the covers with me. I fell back into a deep, restful sleep with my arms wrapped about Cruiser, who was soon snoring along with his adoring mom.

Chapter 36

The following afternoon, I was back at Lakeside Shelter, but this time I wasn't dreaming. Amanda Peabody was at the front desk doing some paperwork on a stray dog that had been brought in. At least it would have a fighting chance for a new home now that Rhoda Marx was gone. A volunteer took over while Amanda and I went into her office.

"My daughter gave me your message."

"Thanks for coming by. I thought you'd be the best person to talk to about this."

"What's going on?"

"There's been some weird stuff going on here."

"Is TAILS up to their old tricks again?"

"Could be. I really don't know. If so, these are some pretty clever tricks."

"What do you mean?"

"Dogs are disappearing."

"Disappearing? You mean someone is letting them out like before?"

"No, I mean I put them in the kennel, and when I go back to the kennel, it's empty. The dog has vanished."

"Dogs don't vanish into thin air. Someone had to have come and let the dog out. Who usually has the keys to the kennels?"

"Rex does. But he's been on vacation, so I keep them in my desk drawer."

"Someone must know where you keep them and is just jerking your choke chain."

"I don't think so. I keep the drawer locked at all times. I'm especially vigilant about it because of what happened before."

"You mean when someone let the dogs out?"

"Someone . . . or something."

"What are you getting at?"

Amanda paused a moment before answering. She knew how what she was going to say would sound to someone else.

"Bertie Finch was right about this place. It should be torn down."

"I tend to agree with her, but why do *you* say that?"

"Because it's haunted, that's why."

"Haunted? By what?" I didn't really have to ask. I think I already knew the answer to that question.

"Gilda's ghost!"

■ ■ ■ ■

I was naturally skeptical of what Amanda had told me about the strange goings-on at the shelter. It seemed more likely that these manifestations were being caused by a two-legged phantom named Tori than a four-legged one named Gilda. But I was intrigued, nevertheless. If dogs were disappearing from the shelter, I felt compelled to find out why.

There was only one way to prove whether or not it was Gilda's ghost that had been causing all the havoc lately at Lakeside Shelter. I'd stay overnight at the shelter and do watchdog duty. Of all the odd jobs I'd done over the years, this had to be one of the oddest. When I told Nona about it, she thought I had flipped my ever-loving beanie. She should know her nutty mother by now — the same one who sees monsters floating in the lake and creatures lurking outside her kitchen window. I couldn't help wondering what I might witness tonight at the haunted animal shelter. Since I wasn't sleeping much lately anyway, there was no reason not to spend the night at Lakeside with Gilda's ghost.

Chapter 37

When I drove into the empty parking lot at Lakeside Shelter, a full moon lit my way to the entrance. I decided to take my crime-busting hound along with me to the shelter, partly as protection but also for his keen CSP (canine sensory perception). Dogs can sense things long before we can, and that was a skill I might need tonight. If anything was amiss or if I was in any danger, he would alert me.

No one but my daughter and Amanda Peabody knew that I would be staying in the shelter overnight. Amanda had given me a key to let myself in. I hadn't worked a graveyard shift since I was in my teens and lasted all of four nights waitressing at a Denny's. I'm no Rita Ramirez, that's for sure. Suffering from sleep deprivation, I dumped a plateload of food in a patron's lap, and that was the end of my brief career as a waitress. I wasn't much of a night owl in those days, but I can hoot with the best of them now.

Cruiser and I entered the shelter, walked past the front office and into the kennel area. Unfortunately, it had quickly filled to capacity again. Most of the escapees had been captured and there were others that had been surrendered since then. Moonbeams spilled through a window at the end of the shelter corridor. I had brought along a flashlight, but the bright moonlight made it unnecessary. I didn't want to announce my presence to anyone.

The inmates were all sound asleep, but when we entered, a dog barked at Cruiser, then another and another. Soon the whole place echoed with the din of barking dogs. Either they were voicing their displeasure that Cruiser was outside and they were on the inside, or they thought I was there to liberate them and were pleading for me to release them from their cages. I hoped they would settle down in a while and go back to sleep. That ghastly noise would be intolerable if it lasted all night long. It might also tip off any would-be intruder that someone was here. Dogs don't bark to hear themselves bark; well, most don't. Calamity was an exception.

Cruiser followed along at my heels as I

passed the kennels, noting the number of dogs contained in each cage so I would know if any were to suddenly go missing while I was there. We came to the kennel that Amanda claimed was haunted. This was formerly Gilda's kennel, from which she said dogs had been mysteriously disappearing. Apparently, she planned on putting her theory to the test since a lone beagle mix was impounded inside the "haunted" kennel.

The cage door was locked to prevent the dog's escape or removal. I thought it rather strange that this was the only dog in the entire place that was not barking its head off. It was huddled in a corner, shivering the same way Calamity had when I found her here. She could be sick, but I didn't think so. The dog's coat was glossy and her eyes clear and bright. She appeared healthy and showed no obvious signs of illness. I recognized a terrified dog when I saw one. As we approached the cage, Cruiser froze in his tracks.

"Come on, Cruiser."

He began to shiver and shake, too.

"Cruiser, come!"

He didn't budge an inch when I commanded him to come to me, which isn't all that unusual, but something else besides stubbornness was causing him to disobey me.

"What is it, boy? What's wrong?"

Cruiser raised his nose to the ceiling and bayed mournfully. Several of the other dogs responded in kind, probably the ones with a bit of hound blood flowing in their veins. That included the beagle mix in K-9. Their eerie vocalizations reminded me of the coyotes I hear in the forest near my cabin on moonlit nights like this one. It always sent a little chill zipping up my spine and caused the hair on my neck to prickle, the same way it was now. Perhaps I was sensing the same thing Cruiser was, for I noticed the ruff of his neck was as spiked as Tori Thatcher's hair.

The din in the shelter was becoming too much to bear. I was starting to get a throbbing headache. With all this uproar, no one was going to make an appearance at the shelter tonight — at least no one living. I decided I'd have to leave Cruiser enclosed in the front office for now. He could do sentry duty there and sound the alarm for me if anyone were to enter the shelter. With his loud, resonant bellow, I'd be certain to hear it clear from the other end of the compound.

I led Cruiser back to the front office and

got him settled down in the dog bed that used to belong to Spirit, the magnificent white shepherd Nona and I had encountered out in the woods. Evidently, the dogcatcher had not recaptured him. He was smart enough to evade capture and by now had probably joined up with some other rogue pack in the woods, assuming he hadn't been hit by a car or come to other harm, as many strays do.

As soon as I took Cruiser out of the kennel area, he stopped his shivering and seemed fine again. The other dogs stopped their barking, too. But suddenly I heard a startling noise. A loud, metallic crash reverberated from somewhere inside the shelter.

"Stay here, Cruiser."

Once more I approached the kennel area, now with some trepidation. I wasn't sure what had caused the noise, but I knew it wasn't one of the dogs. This time I flipped on the lights so I could see what was wrong or surprise whoever might be there. I expected that I might find a certain troublemaker with purple spiked hair making another misguided attempt to focus public attention on the animals' plight on behalf of TAILS. I hurried past the kennels until I came to number 9 again. This time it was I who froze in my tracks. The cage door was thrown wide open and the padlock lay unlocked on the corridor floor. When I peered inside the cage, it was empty. The beagle had vanished into thin air, just as Amanda had described. I looked up and down the corridor for some sign of the missing beagle, and searched every other area of the shelter. There was no sign of her anywhere or any sign of anyone having entered the shelter from outside. Something strange was definitely going on at Lakeside Shelter, and I was more determined than ever to find out what it was.

I was ready to give up the ghost and leave the shelter with Cruiser when I heard a door slam at the farthest end of the building. Cruiser heard it, too. He let out a baritone bark, and when I opened the office door to the kennels he took off tracking at full speed. Tracking what, I had no clue. At least not yet.

Cruiser's alarm was all it took for the Lakeside inmates to be roused from their fitful slumbers and join the barkfest. I had never heard so much noise. How did people work in these places day in and day out and remain sane? If dogs can go kennel crazy after being penned up for so long in shelters with no hope of release from their torment, perhaps people can, too. Is that what had really happened here at Lakeside Shelter? Had one of the shelter workers decided he or she had finally had enough of this stressful job and a hard-nosed boss? Perhaps the Marx woman was the victim of a crazed kennel worker, and she just happened to be in the wrong place at the wrong time. It could also have been a volunteer who might be even more prone to such a psychosis. Volunteers are there because they choose to be. It's not hard to imagine they might be even more inclined to take revenge on someone like her who represented a roadblock to happy endings for the pets at the shelter. From the people I'd spoken to thus far who knew Rhoda, I suspected revenge against her was something that was on the minds of many. The question still remaining was who? Perhaps Cruiser and I were hot on the trail of the killer right now.

I covered my ears to drown out the barking and yelping of the dogs as we passed the kennel rows on our way to the rear of the shelter. Hearing their desperate cries was as distressful to me as hearing a child wailing for its mother. I think it was upsetting Cruiser, too. He understood their language far better than I. What I did understand was why someone had released all the dogs at the shelter, ill advised though it may have been. Part of me wanted to break open every cell door in the place and liberate the dogs from their prison. No one who loves dogs wants to see them end up in a place like this. But there are far worse places to end up besides a shelter. At least in shelters, the animals have a safe place to rest, food and water, medical care, and protection from danger and the elements . . . for a time.

Just as we came to the back door of the shelter, I heard a car engine start up in the rear lot where the animal control vans were parked. I bolted through the door in time to see one of the vehicles backing out of its space. I tried to wave down the person inside the cab, but when he saw me, the van shifted into high gear and sped off. The screeching tires laid a zipper of rubber marks on the pavement. As the van zoomed past me, under the flood of security lights I was able to discern the identity of the driver. It was none other than "Another One Bites the Dust" Rex.

What was he doing skulking around here this late at night? From the looks of things inside the shelter, he hadn't been working overtime cleaning the place. When I heard the distinctive yelps of a hysterical beagle coming from inside the van, I suspected I knew who our mysterious shelter ghost was. What I didn't know was why he was secretly taking animals out of the shelter. And where was he taking them? I decided I had better report this theft to the police immediately. For all I knew, Rex might return, and I wouldn't want him to find me here alone snooping around. I'd already seen how he dealt with animals in the shelter. Right now, I was the one biting Rex's dust from a speeding dogcatcher's van.

Chapter 38

Last-minute preparations for the Bassetille Day event were exactly what I needed to take my mind off of murder and mayhem for a little while. The big day was only a couple of days away, and the Waddle countdown was officially on. There was still plenty to do before the fundraiser, including getting potential adoptees ready to put their best paw forward. In the hope of finding her a new home, Calamity had a date at the groomer to get prettied up, which turned out to be a good thing. For when I got home I discovered that she'd been excavating in my backyard to uncover Cruiser's private reserve, his buried treats, which he liked to age thoroughly before sampling.

Nona had abdicated her pet-sitting duties for the afternoon, so that meant Calamity had enjoyed free reign of the place. She had put her freedom to ample use, indoors and outdoors, as I was about to discover. Fortunately, this pup perp had left plenty of evidence to link her to the crime. All I had to do was follow the muddy paw prints through the house from one end to the other to see what devilment she'd been up to in our absence.

"Cruiser, why didn't you keep her out of trouble while I was gone?" He gave me a sheepish look, which I at first interpreted as being a response to my angry tone of voice until I ascertained that he'd been an accomplice in the caper. I needed look no further for proof than my kitchen. The sight of emptied bags and boxes of treats strewn helter-skelter on the kitchen floor was enough to wrap up this case in short order. Skip might trace his perps with bloodstains, but slobber stains were the trace evidence at this canine crime scene. It was hard to imagine how two short-legged dogs could get into so much mischief in such a short time. But being short dogs did not exclude either Calamity or her cohort, Cruiser, from being prime suspects. Aside from the demolition in my kitchen, this did demonstrate one thing to me: Cruiser and Calamity were definitely beginning to bond with each other, at least long enough to join forces in a pantry raid.

I had begun cleaning up the mess when I

heard Nona pull into the driveway.

Calamity began barking hysterically and ran to the front door to greet her. I wasn't sure whether she was really that happy to see Nona or if she sensed my displeasure with her and was seeking asylum with the one person she had shown any real connection with since coming here. Nona, of course, was completely taken in by that craven little thief.

"Hey, girl, whatcha been up to?" Evidently, she didn't notice the mud on Calamity's paws. If she'd jumped up on her like usual, Nona would have known right off what that naughty dog had been up to.

"Plenty!"

Nona's jaw dropped when she saw the demolition. "Gosh, Mom! What happened in here?"

"What do you think?"

"Calamity did all this?"

"I think she had a little help from her long-eared partner in crime."

"I'm really sorry. I was only gone for a little while. I thought she could be trusted for a few minutes."

"Evidently not. She'll have to be crated from now on if one of us can't be here with her."

"What a naughty girl you are, Calamity!"

Calamity cowered at the sharp tone of Nona's voice. I'm sure it wasn't the first time she'd been yelled at, or worse, for bad behavior.

"It's no good scolding her now, Nona. She doesn't know what you're punishing her for. You'd have to catch her in the act for her to make the connection."

"You're right, but even then I'm not sure it would do any good. This dog is a real hard case."

"Fortunately, she already has a date with the groomer to get prettied up for the Waddle. She'll need to look her best if she's going to get adopted this weekend."

An odd expression clouded Nona's face that I couldn't quite interpret, except that it was similar to the looks she'd given me in the past when I didn't approve of her choice of boyfriends. "Looks like Cruiser could use a little clean-up, too. Why don't you take them both with you while I finish cleaning up the mess here?"

"Thanks, honey. I appreciate that."

I was relieved when Nona agreed to clean up the mess Calamity and Cruiser had made in the house while I took them both to Rub-a-Dub-Dog at Petropolis for a good cleansing. Cruiser hadn't gotten as down and dirty in the yard as Calamity had, so he didn't really need a full bath, but cleanliness is next to doGliness. Even though he wasn't in the market for a new home like Calamity was, I also wanted him to look his best for the Waddle.

I could have tried bathing both the dogs in my bathtub at home, but I knew it would make a worse mess in my house than there already was. I love having dogs, but there are times I wouldn't mind living in a dog-free zone. Tom's mother kept their home so clean, you could have given it the white-glove test at any time. It must have been quite an adjustment for him living with me. I guess I always believed that there were more important things in life than having your house look perfect, and for me a house without a dog is no home. Fortunately, after Cruiser came to live with us, Tom came to share my feelings about that. Keeping Cruiser happy and healthy became paramount at the MacBean abode.

I was starting to think that Nona was taking after her dad in that respect. She was becoming a pretty good sport about all the dog duties she was being asked to perform. Was this the same fussy glamour girl who never let a lock of hair fall out of place and had a hissy fit if she broke a fingernail?

These days she didn't seem to mind getting down and dirty for Cruiser, and especially for Calamity. Was my daughter finally going to the dogs like her mother? I could only hope so. The transformation I was seeing in Nona went much deeper than that, though.

CHAPTER 39

I had actually managed to lead Calamity through the mall to Petropolis and through the door of the pet salon. The fact that Cruiser went along with us was reassuring to her. Despite her errant behavior, the newcomer to the household clearly perceived Cruiser as the alpha of the pack, and his presence had a calming effect upon her. A dog that is confused as to who is leader of the pack is not a well-adjusted dog, and Calamity was undoubtedly the least well-adjusted dog I'd ever encountered.

I even managed to get her into the tub and get her sudsed and partially rinsed without incident. We were doing fine until she heard a blow dryer start up in the next cubicle. She yelped an alarm, snapped her restraint, and bolted out the door of Rub-a-Dub-Dog with me in hot pursuit. I chased after that crazy dog, my hysterical and futile commands echoing all through Petropolis. I worried that she might make it into the main mall and out the front door right into traffic.

Shoppers pointed and laughed at the berserk basset racing through Petropolis covered in foam as though she were rabid. As I ran after her, cursing under my breath, I thought that whoever had named this impossible dog Calamity certainly knew what they were doing. Why no one had ever named a hurricane after her was beyond me.

The soap scum coating Calamity made her as slippery as a greased pig. Twice I nearly nabbed her, but she evaded my grasp each time. My breath came in ragged gasps and I was about to give up the chase when a bystander managed to lasso her with a black leather belt. When I finally caught up with my wayward hound, I realized that the purple-haired basset wrangler was none other than Tori Thatcher. She was there with some of her other rabble-rousers, which made me wonder what trouble they were stirring up at the mall.

"This slippery girl gave you a run for your money, eh?" Tori said, a wry smile lighting her usually stormy countenance.

"No kidding! Thanks for catching her for me." Good thing for Calamity and me that Tori always wore an assortment of leather belts and accessories, including the spiked collar she sported around her neck like a pit bull, only this pit bull wore lipstick.

"Isn't this your latest foster dog from Lakeside?" she said.

"Yes. Her name is Calamity, and that she is."

"Poor girl probably went through a lot before she ended up with you."

"No doubt of that. She definitely has some issues from her past. I wish I knew more about her background, but one rarely knows much about the history of these rescued dogs. Judging from her lack of socialization, I'm fairly certain she was a puppy mill dog."

"And probably a pet shop girl, too," Tori said, stroking one of Calamity's long ears. She gave herself a good shake, showering us both in sudsy water.

"Yep, that's where they usually end up, assuming they survive their deprived puppyhood."

"From the mill to the mall."

"And then to the local shelter after behavior issues surface and the novelty of dog ownership wears off. Discarded like yesterday's newspaper."

"That's part of why we're here today," Tori said, pausing to hand a flyer to a passing shopper. She gave one to me, too. I was right about TAILS being at the mall to stir up trouble, but it was mainly trouble for Lakeside Animal Shelter. They were planning to stage a demonstration to close the facility down for good.

I noticed one detail of the flyer in particular. It so happened that the rally was scheduled on the same day as our Waddle. Was it purely coincidence or had Tori planned it that way? Whether their protest was intended to work in concert with our adoption efforts or to steal our thunder and divert attention to their cause was open to interpretation.

Although Tori claimed to be an advocate for animal rights, her methods always seemed to work at cross purposes to their best interests. She seemed to attract more enemies than allies. I'd seen it happen all too often in other organizations when people's egos are unleashed. The message somehow gets lost before the messenger can deliver it. Whatever Tori did, good or bad, I had come to understand one thing about her. She believed that the ends justified the means if it somehow served the cause of animal welfare. Whether those means had also included murder I had yet to discover.

Chapter 40

The weather was perfect on the day of our first annual Basset Waddle. Tahoe's temperate seventies and a cool breeze would keep the hounds from overheating in their Waddle Wear, which ranged from silly to bizarre. Calamity and other homeless bassets sported green jackets with yellow lettering that read, ADOPT ME! Bassetille Day would go down in Heavenly Valley history as an earmark gathering of basset hounds from hither and yon. Two attendees were real French hounds that had been flown all the way from Paris. *Vive les Bassets!* In all, they were nearly 1,000 strong, long, and ready to waddle.

By the time Nona and I arrived with Cruiser and Calamity in tow, legions of bassets and their owners were already milling about the lakefront dog park getting acquainted.

"I don't know whether it was such a good

idea to bring Calamity along with us, Mom. I'm not sure she's ready for the big time yet."

"There's only one way to find out."

"But she'll probably freak out in the crowd. This dog is still not very well socialized."

"If she isn't socialized after today, then I guess there's no hope for her. Besides, this is her best chance to be placed in a permanent home." I didn't want to say it might also be her last chance, but I didn't have to say it. Nona read between the lines. We both knew the truth was that Calamity had already proved she wasn't a good fit at the MacBean house. A psychotic, destructive dog was more trouble than I could handle in my already complicated life. I could only hope that for this important occasion she'd be on her best behavior, for her sake and mine.

"What do you think the chances are that someone will adopt her today?" Nona said.

"It's hard to say. She's a beautiful dog, and there'll be plenty of hard-core basset lovers here who might be willing to take her on. She may get lucky."

"And what if no one adopts her? What will become of her then?"

"Let's wait and see what happens before

we start worrying about that, okay? Try to think positively. The chances are good that she could find her forever home with someone."

"Perhaps you're right." Nona didn't know it, but I was pretty good at reading between the lines. I knew that she had taken a liking to Calamity from the beginning and that the dog had bonded with her, too. I suspected that Nona was secretly hoping no one would adopt her because she wanted to keep Calamity for herself. There was only one problem with that. Nona lived in a small apartment in San Francisco that didn't allow dogs, at least not dogs her size.

As we entered the dog park, Cruiser took an immediate interest in all the activity. This was an off-leash event, so I unsnapped his lead and let him go his merry way, which he proceeded to do without delay. He lifted his head to the air to sample the buffet of scents wafting past his sensitive nose, then headed off in the direction where hot dogs and hamburgers were being grilled. Calamity had picked up the same delectable scents Cruiser had, but I didn't dare let her off the leash in a crowd this large. I didn't need a repeat of our Petropolis episode. Besides, it was Nona's job to lead her around and make sure everyone knew that she was available for adoption.

"It looks like you have things in hand here with Calamity. Walk her around the park and let's hope someone takes a shine to her. Maybe you can enter her in some of the contests to showcase her a bit. She'd be a shoo-in for the longest ears competition."

"Great idea! Sounds like fun."

"I have to take my shift now in the Found Hounds booth. Keep an eye on Cruiser for me, will you? He's waddling around here somewhere."

"Sure." I watched as Nona led Calamity off among the crowd. Almost immediately an elderly couple took interest in her. Calamity seemed a bit hesitant at first about all the attention she was getting, but Nona's presence was reassuring to her. A couple of treats didn't hurt, either. The surest way to a basset's heart is through its stomach, as the assortment of belly draggers at this event proved without a doubt. The more attention Calamity could get here, the better. Even if she didn't leave the Waddle with a new family, she would come away with some new experiences, and that was good for an unsocialized dog like her.

Found Hounds had set up their booth in the dog park along with an assortment of vendors selling sundry basset-a-bilia and everything from leashes and collars to doggy designer duds and snoods for keeping long ears from dipping in food bowls. Calamity's ears could sure use one of those. It would probably be helpful for the infections that are inherent with the extreme breeding practices that continue to produce exaggerated features like those ridiculously lengthy ears of hers. Whoever adopted Calamity would have their work cut out for them with her, in more ways than that. Luckily, the kinds of people this type of function attracts are already familiar with the breed and its inherent challenges, but they love them anyway.

At the Found Hounds booth I handed out flyers, brochures, and other materials to educate folks about the organization. Our booth was located in the animal health and welfare section, right next to TAILS! I felt it was poor event organization to set up a booth for them right next to us, but I tried to make the best of the situation. Their volunteers were so aggressive with their animal rights spiel that I was beginning to feel like a sideshow barker, if you'll forgive the pun. But the one barking the loudest was Tori the Terrible, who had arrived on the scene. Even if I didn't approve of her methods, I had to admit that she was a force to be reckoned with on behalf of the animals. She certainly put her all into anything she did.

"Tori, I didn't expect to see your group at this event."

"We couldn't pass up a crowd of this size to get the word out."

"Who signed you up for the Waddle?"

"Jenna Fairbanks, why?"

"Your organization is probably too radical for a breed-specific fun event like this."

"I was under the impression you're also trying to place some homeless dogs here in adoptive homes."

"Yes, we are."

"Then I think our message is certainly *à propos.*"

Now she was hurling fancy French words at me, which I guess was *à propos* at an event for French dogs. I just hoped that Tori, whose middle name is trouble, wasn't here to stir up some.

CHAPTER 41

It was time for some grub when my stomach roared louder than Tori Thatcher. That woman's voice was like the sound of broken glass in a cement mixer. She sure didn't need a megaphone to make her point. Tori had missed her true calling as a carnival barker, but I had to admit she was good at getting people fired up for her cause.

She was busy talking with so many other people she didn't have much time to spend talking to me, but there are other ways besides that to gather valuable information about someone. As any dog would tell you if he had the power of speech, people communicate their intentions far more accurately without words. A dog can tell you what you're feeling even before you're aware of it yourself. Body language and other forms of nonverbal communication speak volumes about humans. Tori's alpha essence emanated from every pore of her stocky body. Even I sensed that. Clearly, there was much more to her than met the eye of the casual observer, but you could say that about most anyone if you studied the person carefully enough. People can be a bit like assorted candies. A hard shell can encase a gooey soft center, or sometimes there's a tough nut buried inside a deceptively smooth, creamy coating.

Jenna Fairbanks approached my booth toting an armload of leaflets.

"Here to replenish my stock?"

"Yes. How are things going?" She brushed away a stray flaxen lock of hair.

"All right. I think I'm about ready for a break, though. Can you cover for me while I eat a bite?"

"Actually, I was about to relieve you. They want you over in the ring to help judge some of the contests."

"What kind of contests?"

"Oh, they have several categories: longest ears, lowest ground clearance, best trick, best treat catch, to name a few."

"That should be a hoot!"

I spotted Nona heading for my booth with Calamity hot on her heels. I figured I could send her for provisions, but she was way ahead of me.

"I thought you must have been getting

hungry by now, Mom. All they had were hot dogs and hamburgers."

"No veggie burgers, huh?"

"Nope, sorry. I brought you a regular burger, though."

"If that's all they have, I guess I'll have to bend my dietary rules for the occasion. I'm starving!"

Apparently, I wasn't the only one. If I were a flea on Calamity's back, I might have noticed that her doggy radar was tracking Nona's every move with that burger. There's nothing quite as keen as the nose of a basset hound, and hers was certainly no exception, as I had already discovered on several occasions.

I have Calamity to thank for keeping me vegetarian in spite of myself. I was so hungry I would have gladly gobbled down every bit of that burger if she hadn't beat me to it. As I chatted with Jenna, she saw her chance and took advantage of the distraction. The hamburger, on a paper plate near my elbow and a little too near the edge of the table, disappeared in one gulp. She'd devoured half the paper plate too, before I realized what had happened. Even David Copperfield couldn't make anything vanish into thin air as quickly as Calamity snatched that burger right from under my nose. The paw is quicker than the eye.

"Bad girl!" It was no good protesting. My burger had already disappeared down the biscuit hole. I tugged at the paper plate to retrieve it before the rest of it was gone, but she fought me with every ounce of her will. Finally, rather than lose a digit, I gave in and let her have what was left of my white plate special. A little paper pulp was nothing compared to what else she'd ingested so far since joining my household, and she'd survived that with no trouble.

"She's a little food guarder, isn't she?" Jenna said.

"I'm afraid so. She's never nipped me, but it's probably because the hand's been quicker than the tooth thus far. I'm not sure I'd trust this dog around small children. She might not be able to discern the difference between baby fingers and Snausages."

"That's too bad. A behavior fault like that may limit her chances for adoption."

"You're probably right. This one slipped through the screening process, or I wouldn't even have her."

"Rhoda Marx would never have let that happen. I saw her fail perfectly adoptable dogs for much less than food-guarding."

"That must have bothered you."

"Yes, but not as much as it bothered Bertie, who lost Gilda to Rhoda's inflexible policies. No one hated that woman as much as she did."

"I guess it's fortunate for Calamity that Rhoda wasn't at the shelter the day I came for her. She would probably have ended up the same way Gilda did. I guess no one misses Rhoda Marx much, but I'm not sure she deserved to die like a dog."

"I'm sorry about what happened to Rhoda, but the truth is things have been better for the shelter since she's been gone. In fact, most of the dogs up for adoption at this event wouldn't be here today if she were still around. She saw euthanizing pets as the quickest, least costly solution to overpopulation. She actually seemed to relish her reputation for efficiency in carrying out those distasteful duties."

"In her way, she may have thought she was doing the right thing."

"Are you defending her?"

"Of course not, but the fact remains that she was responsible for running a small, overcrowded shelter with a limited budget in a community overrun with strays. As Rex said, there's only so much space for homeless pets in the shelter. I'm sure her decisions weren't easy ones."

"They weren't, but she never seemed to have any trouble making them. Rhoda would have made a good prison matron, but she was ill-suited to her job as shelter manager and should have been replaced a long time ago."

"Seems to be the consensus. Obviously, someone wanted her out of there, by whatever method."

"Murder is a pretty drastic method, though, even for someone like Rhoda."

"Who do you think killed her?"

A maelstrom swirled in Jenna's sea green eyes as she pondered my question. I think its bluntness caught her off guard. I'm usually good at reading people, especially when I look into their eyes, which truly are the windows of the soul, but I could not quite determine the emotion I was seeing within hers. She had worked with Rhoda and expressed regret for her fate. Whether that regret was genuine was hard to determine. If anyone who'd had any dealings with Rhoda felt sad about her demise, I had not seen any evidence of it yet. At length, Jenna spoke, and her answer surprised me. "I think we are all responsible for what happened to Rhoda."

"Really? How so?"

"Because we allowed her to remain in

control of the shelter and let her polices go unchallenged, even though we knew she was all wrong for the shelter, the community and especially the animals in her care. Everyone despised her. It was only a matter of time before someone took matters into their own hands."

Jenna was right. Anyone who knew Rhoda's reputation at the shelter and remained silent was as guilty as the one who put her inside that chamber and turned on the gas. Only one question remained: Who actually killed the dog killer?

CHAPTER 42

I hadn't been having much fun thus far at the Waddle, so I was grateful to be relieved from booth duty to help judge the talent contest. Having such a contest for basset hounds would probably not be much of a competition, I figured, since the main talents I've seen in bassets are sleeping and eating. Well, a little sleuthing too, in Cruiser's case.

I was selected to judge the Best Howl and Best Trick competitions. The dog that won the prize for Best Trick was the only one that actually performed a trick on command, and I had to admit it was a good one. Sonny's owner had taught him how to paint. With a tennis player's terrycloth wristband placed on the dog's paw, he dipped the terry "brush" in paint, then held up a blank sheet of paper for his dog. Of course, there was a treat involved in the performing of this trick. Upon hearing the repeated command, "Paint!" Vincent van Basset did his artistic stuff. What he painted was up for interpretation, but it looked about as good as some modern art I've seen exhibited in galleries. Regardless, it was a clever trick, and he was the paws-down winner of the contest.

Other categories were the Best Treat Catch and Counter Surfing competitions. Calamity had already unofficially claimed the counter surfing title with her Houdini disappearing hamburger act. Anyone who had happened to witness her agility on the table where I was momentarily distracted from my lunch couldn't argue that this was the fastest-moving basset they'd seen at the Waddle, or anywhere else. There were also competitions for longest body; lowest ground clearance, measured tummy to turf; and longest wingspan, where long ears were measured tip-to-tip while extending them like Dumbo the flying elephant's.

This was Calamity's big moment in the ring. Nona led the contestant into the competition circle to join a group of other bassets with very long ears. Now, anyone who knows this breed is aware of the original purpose of those low-hanging ears, and it has nothing to do with dog shows or competitions of any kind. If you were to watch a basset hound running in slow motion, which is poetry for any basset lover, you'd see the gentle flapping of the ears as the dog runs, nose to the ground. That flapping motion stirs up scents, which are trapped in folds inside that ultra-sensitive nose of his. Of course, the one scent that would hold particular interest for a basset is rabbit, which is what he was especially bred to track for the hunter following him on foot. It's easy to see that ears so long the dog trips on them while running are pretty useless for hunting purposes, but they are perfect for contests like the one being held at the Waddle.

One contestant for the longest ears contest wore a snood, which is customary at Westminster and other conformation dog shows for keeping ears clean and tidy before entering the judging ring. They help prevent ears from dragging on the ground and keep bacteria from collecting in ears that are already the perfect breeding grounds for infection since not much air gets into the dog's ear canals. Cruiser's ears had never been much of a problem because they are not exceptionally long or heavy, but Calamity's were the opposite and would always be troublesome for whoever adopted her. I was hoping that she might win the longest ears contest, not for any award she might win but because being showcased in the winner's circle was sure to grab the attention of a potential adopter.

"Come on, girls, do your stuff," I cheered as Nona and Calamity entered the arena of long-eared contestants.

Nona looked rather proud as she extended Calamity's ears to their full breadth as the judge wielded his tape across her "wingspan" for the official measurement. Since pairs of ears can vary in length, each ear was measured individually and the numbers combined.

"We have a total of 27.25 inches for Calamity. That matches the world record holder."

"Woo, hoo!" Nona yelled. Calamity leapt for joy because she understood from Nona's reaction that she had pleased the one who was clearly becoming the object of affection for a dog that had not had much of the same in her short life.

"Hooray for Calamity!" All the spectators were cheering and applauding for her, and she was eating it all up with more enthusiasm than she'd earlier exhibited for an unguarded hamburger. Could this be the key to Calamity that I'd been missing all along? Perhaps all she really needed was to be the center of attention for a change. Who knew what she had experienced before she ended up at Lakeside Shelter or what positive reinforcement she had been denied in her young life? Certainly, there had been a lack of love. She had much in common with many humans who seek attention because they never had enough of it in their early lives. They derive that attention through acting out in negative ways or becoming the clown. This dog used both to get the attention she craved. But her moment of adulation was over, at least for now. The longest ears competition wasn't quite over. There was still one more competitor remaining who might measure up to Calamity, and his name was Longfellow.

When the un-neutered male basset waddled into the ring, it was immediately evident how Longfellow may have acquired his name. You wanted to believe it was because of the length of his body or his ears . . . until you got the view of his undercarriage. Fortunately, no one would be measuring anything else on the dogs today, but I was guessing that Longfellow must have already prevailed in the Lowest Ground Clearance contest.

You could almost have heard the familiar strains of Strauss's "Also Sprach Zarathustra" rising to its Odysseyan crescendo when Longfellow's snood finally came off and the dog's prodigious ears unfurled in all their glory. The dog was already so low in stature that his ears dragged the ground when he walked, causing him to trip and stumble. Everyone laughed, but I felt a strong urge to track down the insane breeder who was responsible for these mutant ears and strangle him or her with them. What on earth do you do with ears like those except keep them folded up in a silly snood until the next longest ears contest? We were all about to find out the answer to that question. A dramatic hush fell over the crowd as Longfellow's voluminous ears were extended horizontally to their full breadth. No one had ever seen ears that long on a basset before, except perhaps in a Berkley Breathed cartoon. One good gust of wind and the dog would have taxied down the dog park for take-off.

The judge measured first one ear and then the other. He was taking so long to confirm the measurement that at first I thought it was only for dramatic effect, but it was really only to recheck his numbers for accuracy. He gaped in amazement. Evidently, even he couldn't believe what he was seeing on the tape measure. At long last he spoke to the crowd, who clearly couldn't believe what they were seeing, either.

"Fellow Waddlers, the official winner of the Longest Ears contest is Longfellow." And this time he did pause for dramatic effect before making his next announcement. "At a total length of 30.5 inches, we have an entry for the *Guinness Book of World Records.* Mr. Jeffries the basset hound and Tigger the bloodhound have been bested for the world's longest ears. Congratulations, Longfellow!"

The crowd went wild, but the victor seemed unimpressed by all the attention he was getting. Perhaps there was good reason for his *laissez faire.* After all, he was the one who had to live with those bothersome ears day in and day out, tripping over them, having them stepped on, dragging them in his food and water bowls. The truth was, Longfellow was far more interested in sniffing the nearest tree trunk, where he left a message for the contestants in the next competition and grand finale to the Waddle . . . Best Howl. This would be Cruiser's moment to shine, because everyone knew that there was no better howler in all of Lake Tahoe than my crooning Caruso, Cruiser.

CHAPTER 43

The commotion from the howling competition finally subsided, and Cruiser was polishing off the remaining crumbs of his victory biscuit. His reigning title as Best Howler had prevailed despite some truly impressive vocalizing, including the people, who were hoarse from coaxing their dogs to howl loudest and longest. If South Tahoe residents didn't know there was a Basset Hound Waddle under way from all that caterwauling, they soon would.

It was time to waddle down Lake Tahoe Boulevard, not only to show off our dogs dressed in their best Waddle Wear but also to raise the public's awareness of the plight of homeless pets and the need for a modern, no-kill shelter in the community. Along the way, other people with their dogs of all breeds joined the march until our numbers were truly formidable.

Tori and her placard-toting gang, who had

infiltrated our parade, joined in the procession despite a few protests from Found Hounds members. Some people didn't like the fact that their posters were such in-your-face, graphic statements about the evils of animal neglect and cruelty. This wasn't exactly the image we wanted to project to the public for our first annual Bassetille Day Waddle. We naturally wished to garner support for our cause, but this day was meant for fun and celebration of the dogs, and of course, to find good homes for some of them. There wasn't much we could really do to keep Tori and her storm troopers from joining in our Thousand Hound March. Last time I checked, it was still a free country, and freedom of speech is an inalienable right for TAILS as much as it is for Found Hounds.

Leading the march through town was the Jowl-flappers Float with a banner proclaiming the hoards of waddling hounds to follow. The float carried the two dogs that had been crowned as Waddle King and Queen. Those honors were reserved for dogs that had survived despite all odds against them to be adopted into permanent homes and live out their remaining years happily with people who understood them and showered them with all the love and attention every dog deserves.

The Waddle King, named Subway, still bore deep facial scars from the barbed wire his former owner had used to wire his mouth shut to keep him from howling. The scars looked like tears on his muzzle. It had taken him a long time to rediscover his loud and beautiful voice, and he was using it today with gusto. He seemed to understand that this was a special celebration of him and his fellow hounds.

Sharing the float with Subway were the winners of the various contests, including Longfellow, Cruiser, and also the winner of the costume contest, a Basset Boeing 747, wearing a body stocking with Styrofoam wings glued to the airplane fuselage. The float also served as a Saggin' Wagon for a couple of senior hounds with health issues who couldn't keep pace with the pack. The other thousand or so dogs followed the float, at varying rates of speed, or lack thereof, led by their proud owners, some of whom deserved prizes of their own for silliest costume.

Other doggy attire consisted of goofy hats or ready-made costumes purchased at Petropolis or the Haute Hydrant. With the exception of several dogs that shook off their chapeaux quicker than a basset does anything except eat, most of the dogs were good sports about being dressed up for the amusement of others and didn't seem to mind being the focus of all the cheering, jeering spectators lined up along the Waddle route.

As we made our way at snail's pace down Lake Tahoe Boulevard, leaving a slime trail of basset drool in our wake, people spilled out of the tourist shops at Heavenly Village to gape at the spectacle and laugh at the funny dogs in dress-up. We didn't mind the ridicule, as long as we got a new shelter and more adoptive homes for dogs like these. Reno might have its low-riders on Hot August Nights, but South Tahoe had its own version of low-riders on Bassetille Day.

Everything was going smoothly enough with our pup parade and our colorful banners about building a new shelter in Tahoe. Then spectators got an eyeful of the graphic placards. No one really wants reminding of the result of puppy mills and people's failure to spay and neuter their pets, and certainly not in the way TAILS chose to get the message across. Mothers shielded their children's eyes, and others averted their gaze. One guy actually threw up, but it wasn't clear whether the cause was the offensive signage or one too many drinks in the casinos.

Tori's troops already had earned a reputation in the community as troublemakers, having been blamed for various acts of vandalism and even a fire that broke out at a pet store accused of selling puppies from Midwest puppy mills. Whether or not TAILS was really responsible for everything they got blamed for hadn't yet been proved, but they were guilty by association. As their group passed by, some people in the crowd turned and walked away, disgusted. Others shouted and hurled insults at those carrying signs, particularly at Tori, who was an irresistible target with her Goth attire and purple spiked hair. You had to wonder if she liked the attention she got with that hair and all the rest of what made Tori Thatcher who she was, even if it was mostly negative.

We had nearly made it through the entire Waddle route down Lake Tahoe Boulevard when a spectator stepped out from among the crowd and ripped the placard Tori carried from her hand.

"Someone should euthanize you, you freak!" he shouted.

Tori snatched at the sign, but the spectator struck her over the head with it. Another member leapt to her defense, and the aggressor's buddy leapt to his. Others in the parade joined in the fray, and the dogs began baying in discordant chorus their excitement and distress over their humans behaving badly. Despite my own negative attitude about Tori and company, their demonstration had been peaceful. I couldn't stand idly by and watch them be harmed in a preemptive attack. I soon found myself right in the middle of an all-out dogfight.

Dogs waddled at will as leashes were released in the midst of the mêlée. Several dogs broke out in fights. Never in the history of Lake Tahoe had anyone witnessed anything like the grand finale of the first annual Bassetille Day Waddle. Not since the French Revolution had there been a protest march to rival this one, at least one with a pack of unruly French dogs. No one from the casinos was making any bets on who would win the battle for the boulevard, but all bets were off when the police arrived, wielding their batons. With their sensitive noses, the hounds were no doubt grateful that the cops didn't use pepper spray, too!

CHAPTER 44

It didn't take long for the law to subdue the crowd run amok. The sight of uniforms and riot gear quickly took the fight out of them, and no one got the business end of the baton, except for the guy who had whacked Tori with her own protest sign. He was taken into custody, and the officer doing the cuffing was none other than Skip's protégé, Rusty Cannon. She might have been small in stature, but there was nothing small about her attitude, as I'd already discovered on more than one occasion. Meanwhile, other officers took the opportunity to round up several drunks for a ride in the paddy wagon.

Once the Waddle attendees and lookie-loos began to disperse, the event was officially concluded. Those who had participated in the parade turned to the business of collecting their wayward hounds. With nose-blind bassets, that might be even more of a challenge than gaining public support for a new shelter was turning out to be. I spotted another familiar face among the officers who were busy restoring peace in the Valley of the Dogs.

"Skip, am I glad to see you!"

"Beanie, what the heck are you doing in the middle of this fracas?"

"It wasn't by choice, I assure you. We were just trying to have a fun day out at our first Tahoe Basset Waddle, and we would have if it hadn't turned into a mob scene."

"It may be your last Basset Waddle if they all end up like this one."

"If Tori Thatcher has anything to do with it, you mean. She never misses an opportunity for advancing her TAILS agenda."

"She and that bunch of wackos are starting to make such a bad name for themselves in this community, I'll have to keep a closer eye on their activities from now on."

Speaking of keeping an eye on things, I'd completely lost track of my own dog in all the confusion. The Jowl Flappers float was now devoid of dogs, except for a couple of senior hounds who were too old or blind to find their way around without assistance. I saw no sign of Cruiser there, though, or anywhere among the other hounds that had waddled in the parade. Where, oh where, had my basset hound gone?

"Skip, have you seen Cruiser?"

"No, but he must be wandering around here somewhere. He can't have gone far."

"That's what you think. You know that dog has the wanderlust. How do you think I ended up with him in the first place?"

"I'd like to help you look for him, but as you can see I've got my hands full right now. Isn't Nona here with you?"

"I've lost track of her too, in all the confusion."

"Well, go find her. Maybe she has him."

"I hope so. They'll be letting the traffic through on the boulevard soon. Bassets have no road sense whatsoever."

"Don't worry, Beanie. You'll find him. Think like Cruiser. Where would he be most likely to go?"

I pondered that question only a moment when the answer became obvious. Where does a basset go? Where there's food, of course. "Thanks, Skip. I know just where to look for him."

I headed for the spot I felt sure I'd find Cruiser. Fortunately, I remembered passing a hot dog stand earlier along the parade route. Where else would you expect to find a hungry hound dog? Cruiser had been hanging around the barbecue at the Waddle earlier where hamburgers and hot dogs were being cooked. I'd caught him nabbing wieners from unwary tots, leaving them bawling while holding empty hot dog buns. That is, when he wasn't being offered treats from folks who couldn't resist that artful beggar basset of mine. At a Basset Waddle, soft touches for treats are always in abundance.

I found the hot dog stand, all right, but no Cruiser. The dog mom in me was beginning to panic, especially after a steady stream of traffic had resumed its busy course along Lake Tahoe Boulevard. He is pretty smart, but he's still a basset, and no basset's keen nose is immune to leading him straight into trouble. I was glad that Tom wasn't around to witness this disaster. He would have been very upset with me for letting Cruiser out of my sight, even for a second. Nona wasn't too happy with me either, when she finally appeared with Calamity, safely tethered on her leash. I was proud of Nona for taking good care of her charge. I, however, had broken the first commandment of dog safety: Love 'em and leash 'em. Calamity would have been long gone if she'd been let off her leash, but I'd trusted Cruiser. He'd been with me a long time, but it was trust apparently undeserved.

"Dad would be furious with you for losing his dog."

"No need to remind me of that. I should never have let him off his leash, but the Waddle was an off-leash event. I thought he'd be safe on the float with the other dogs and people, but I didn't expect all hell to break loose. After all this time, I thought I could rely on Cruiser not to wander away from me."

"Now you know better."

"We have to keep looking for him. He can't have gotten that far in such a short time. That inquisitive sniffer of his is bound to slow him down some, especially if he encounters any tasty tidbits along the way."

"Maybe Calamity can help us track him down. She has a keen sniffer, too."

I wasn't placing any bets on Calamity to provide any assistance in our search for Cruiser, but it was worth a try. "I guess we can use all the help we can get. The sooner we find Cruiser, the better the chance he won't get into trouble."

"Come on, girl. Let's go find Cruiser!"

In response to Nona's command, Calamity dropped her nose to the ground as though it was magnetized. She shifted into warp waddle and bayed so loudly it surprised even her. Had she picked up his scent so quickly? She seemed to understand that this was a bona fide hound dog emergency. Even in the short time she had lived with us, she had bonded with Cruiser well enough to recognize what constituted a full pack in my home. It was evident even to crazy Calamity that an important member of the MacBean pack was missing and must be located without delay.

CHAPTER 45

Calamity tugged at her tether like a team of huskies in the Iditarod, with Nona and me following her lead in our frantic search for Cruiser. We queried everyone we passed along the way as to the whereabouts of my wayward hound but got no leads. No one had seen a dog matching his description or any bassets at all since the parade had ended. All hounds were accounted for, except mine.

We searched for him until nightfall made it impossible to continue. I didn't want to give up, but it was no use with dark coming on. When we were just about to rein in Calamity's search and rescue effort, she froze at the entrance to a Pay & Park lot. She read the pavement with her nose like it was basset Braille, then let out a howl and dragged us into the lot. She led us right to a vacant parking space, flopped down on her haunches and bayed at the rising moon. I already knew she was a strong contender in the best howl competition, but I'd never heard her carry on like this before. It was clear that she had brought us to the end of the scent trail, or at least as far as she was able to follow it. There was no sign of Cruiser in the parking lot, but I had a strong sense that this was the last place he'd been. So did Calamity. What no one knew was where he'd gone from here.

My distress over not having found Cruiser was matched by that of Nona and Calamity. As we loaded the young dog into her crate and reluctantly headed for home, even she seemed aware that something was wrong because Cruiser wasn't coming home with us, too. I brushed away tears as I thought about Cruiser wandering the streets of South Lake Tahoe, the same as when Tom discovered him one summer's end wandering starved and lost. I hoped he hadn't survived that trauma and more only to end up under the wheels of a car on Lake Tahoe Boulevard or some other busy road before I could rescue him all over again. Calamity heard me crying, and her anguished cries of distress echoed mine from the back of the car.

"Don't worry, Mom. Cruiser's a pretty street-wise dog. He knows how to avoid traffic. He did before, didn't he?"

"True."

"I'm sure he'll be okay. Someone may have already picked him up."

"Could be. If that's the case, I hope it was the right kind of person who'll attend to his welfare until I can reclaim him." It seemed like a strong possibility Cruiser had caught a ride with someone, especially since Calamity had tracked him to a parking lot. The only thing that worried me was who might have picked up my long-eared hitchhiker. Was it another basset lover or had the dogcatcher found him first?

At least I knew it couldn't be Round 'em Up Rhoda. Of course, there was the possibility it could be her protégé, Rex. Fortunately, Doc Heaton had microchipped Cruiser, so his identification could be easily traced if someone did find him. That and his ID tag were his best insurance of being returned safely to his home.

"He's got to be somewhere in Tahoe. He can't have gotten too far on those stubby legs of his. We'll post some signs tomorrow and place an ad in the paper. Someone is bound to have seen a handsome fellow like him wandering around town."

I knew Nona was trying to keep things light for my benefit, but she was right about one thing. A comical-looking basset hound doesn't usually go unnoticed for long. Surely, someone would find Cruiser before any harm could befall him. But I also worried about all the dogs that had been disappearing from the shelter. The night I saw someone abscond with the beagle, I knew that something sinister was afoot. The possibility that Cruiser might end up in a research lab or as bully bait was too horrid a prospect to consider.

When we arrived home, Calamity explored every room in the house, but for once she wasn't interested in looking for mischief to get into. She was clearly intent on searching for her pack mate, Cruiser. Once she'd made her rounds of the cabin and discovered that there was no other dog on the premises, she slunk to her snuggly bed in the living room, where she curled up, giving me the sagging, mournful look that only a basset hound can. Such a countenance surely must have inspired Shakespeare to write his tragedies. After all, Will did pen verse about bassets. "Ears that sweep away the morning dew; slow in pursuit, but matched in mouth like bells" — what else could the bard have been describing but a basset hound? Calamity's Hershey's kiss eyes, accented with prominent whites and cherry red haws for effect, spoke the same sad query we all were thinking that night: Where is Cruiser?

I felt a glimmer of hope when, upon arriving home, I noticed the blinking red light on my phone indicating that someone had left a message. Nona was right. Someone had found Cruiser and mercifully had wasted no time dialing the number engraved on his trusty dog tag, the first line of defense in insuring the quick return of a lost dog. There was also a better chance of reclaiming an older dog like Cruiser than a puppy. People were not so inclined to part with a pup, especially a purebred, but finding a large senior dog that could eat you out of house and home and cost you a bundle in vet bills was usually a guaranteed return ticket for the dog's swift trip home. In this respect, Cruiser's age was in his favor. At least he hadn't gone missing in the dead of winter. Even the coyotes found it hard surviving snowbound Tahoe winters.

I wasted no time in playing back the phone message. It was about Cruiser, all right. I was crestfallen to learn that it was only Skip checking to see if we'd found him, but the second part of his message was even more disturbing. He told me Roberta Finch had been found dead at the Basset Waddle.

CHAPTER 46

In his message, Skip had neglected to mention the cause of Bertie's death. Theoretically, this unexpected turn of events should have narrowed my field of suspects in the ongoing Marx murder investigation. Who hated Rhoda worse than Bertie had or wanted as badly to get even with her? Just about everyone who hated Rhoda Marx would have been at the Waddle. Was Bertie now also a victim of the killer? Why? I called Skip right back but got no answer and had to leave a message for him, too.

"Skip, it's Beanie. I got your message. Thanks for calling to check on Cruiser. We haven't found him yet. I was hoping you were someone calling to say they had. Nona and I will resume our search first thing tomorrow. Keep an eye out for my boy, okay? I'm worried sick about him. Terrible news about Bertie Finch. I need to talk to you about that as soon as possible."

When I hung up the phone, I noticed that the red light was still on. Someone had left a new message while I was returning Skip's call. This time I hoped it was the call I was waiting for, that someone had found Cruiser and he was safe in their keeping until I could bring him home again. I played it back.

"Elsie, it's Jenna. We found Cruiser. He's here at the shelter, and it's about to close. Better hurry!"

I didn't call her back. No time to waste. I passed Nona and Calamity on my way out the door. Nona sensed the urgency. So did Calamity, but she probably just thought it was time for her walk.

"Someone has found Cruiser, Mom?"

"Yes. That was Jenna Fairbanks. He's turned up at Lakeside Shelter. Thank goodness he's safe!"

"Want us to come along?"

"No, it's okay. It might upset Calamity to be around the shelter again. You stay here and keep your dog company."

I anticipated a retort at my suggestion that Calamity was Nona's dog, but the only response I got was, "Okey-dokey." I think all three of us understood now whose dog Calamity was, especially Calamity herself.

I snatched my sweater from the hall tree

as I left. Summer evenings at Tahoe often turn chilly. Excused from having to join the search for lost dogs, Nona curled up with a book in her father's old easy chair as Calamity made herself comfy on the ottoman. "All right, you two. I'll be back in a jiffy from the pound with my found hound."

When I drove up to Lakeside's entrance, the shelter was pitch dark except for a streetlight in the lot. I expected that Jenna would be waiting for me with Cruiser up front, but the lights were out in the office, too. Perhaps she'd had to leave before I arrived, but she'd left the door unlocked, so I let myself in.

Light spilled down the hallway from the rear of the shelter, so I followed it, assuming she must be attending to something back in the kennel area. When I got there, though, I saw no sign of Jenna or my dog. I was beginning to get a funny feeling about this. Something didn't seem quite right to me, and that feeling was affirmed when I heard Cruiser let out a mournful howl.

I had lived with my dog long enough to recognize every nuance of his canine language, and this was without any doubt a howl of distress. Like a mother responding to the cry of her child, I bolted through the shelter, all the way down the gray mile to the place from where the sound seemed to originate. I hoped I wasn't going to find Jenna in the same condition as I'd found her boss, Rhoda, but my main concern right now was to locate my dog as quickly as possible. As I drew closer, I noticed that Cruiser's cries sounded distant or muffled, as though he was barking from inside a box. My anxiety grew tenfold when my frantic search for Cruiser led me right to the door of the euthanasia room.

When I thrust open the door, I was horrified to discover Cruiser trapped inside the death chamber. Now I understood why his vocalizations had sounded so strangely distant. When he saw me enter the room, his loud howls for help subsided to a pitiful whimper.

"Cruiser! What on earth are you doing in there, boy?"

Thank goodness I had arrived in time. Unlike in my nightmare, he was still alive. I had no idea why he was locked inside the deadly contraption, or who would have put him in it, but I wasted no time in getting him out. Fortunately, no one had turned the thing on while he was in there. I unlatched the death chamber door to free my dog, but as I did, Cruiser grumbled a warning. I instinctively knew he wasn't growling at me but at something else. By the time I realized the peril I was in, it was too late to defend myself. I felt a sudden jerk and something tightening sharply around my neck until I was gasping for breath. My last thought before my world went black was what the kennel attendant Rex had said about "choking out" cats with the catch-pole.

CHAPTER 47

When I regained consciousness, the first thing I became aware of was the sound of Cruiser barking his head off. My throat was sore from the constriction with the choke pole that had been used to subdue me.

I was still so dazed that at first I didn't know exactly where I was, but I knew it wasn't where I should be, at home safe and sound with Nona and my Cruiser. When I saw Jenna Fairbanks peering in at me through the viewing panel of the CO chamber, I realized I was in a tight spot, in more than one way. She had lured me here to Lakeside Shelter with my own dog! Was he only bait for this trap, or had she really meant to kill Cruiser? Why would she do that?

It appeared she had the same fate in mind for me. If it had been Tori Thatcher out there instead of Jenna, I wouldn't have been so befuddled by my desperate situation. I could more easily have believed Tori capable of such a dastardly deed, but Jenna was on our team, wasn't she? My earlier inklings about her had been correct, after all, because it was becoming uncomfortably clear that Jenna meant me grave harm. Exactly why was still unclear, but not for long. She was about to do me the favor of enlightening me of her motives before flipping the switch. I suppose she figured I wouldn't be telling anyone what she was about to tell me.

At least I was the only one inside here now. There was some comfort in knowing that Cruiser was safe in a holding cell across the room. He was barking hysterically because he knew I wasn't safe and he was powerless to come to my aid. Neither could Skip. He couldn't know the danger I was in. Neither of my crime-fighting comrades would be dashing to my rescue this time.

"I'm sorry to have to do this, Elsie, but you really leave me no alternative."

"You don't have to do this, Jenna."

"Yes, I do. I have no choice now. You were getting too close to the truth about what happened to Rhoda Marx, and I can't go to prison. What would happen to my dogs? They're my responsibility, you see. There aren't enough good homes for all of them."

When she talked of her dogs, I understood that she was referring to all the Found Hounds she rescued that were still in need of adoptive homes. But I also understood that the Milkbones had finally spilled out of Jenna's biscuit jar. The woman was clearly seriously disturbed.

I tried to remain as calm as I could under the circumstances. I was going to have to do my best to talk my way out of this situation. Fortunately, I'd learned a few tricks from Skip about calming a potentially violent suspect and defusing difficult situations. This one definitely qualified.

"I understand exactly how you feel about the dogs, Jenna. I feel the same way."

"I didn't mean to kill Rhoda, but you just couldn't reason with that woman. She threatened to euthanize Gilda because she was old and her owner couldn't come to claim her immediately. She could have waited one more day and spared Gilda, but her attitude was that senior dogs can never be placed, so you'd best save the county money and dispatch them as quickly as possible."

No wonder they called her Mengele Marx and Lakeside was considered a canine concentration camp. As a devoted dog lover, I understood Jenna's, and everyone else's, feelings about Rhoda, but that still didn't justify murder.

I was starting to feel like I was a priest inside a confessional listening to a sinner seeking absolution, but no priest ever heard a confession from inside a chamber like this one!

"Gilda had a home and someone who loved her," Jenna continued, "but Rhoda killed her just to be her usual nasty self and assert her power over all of us like the miserable control freak she was. She tried to block every adoption, so we had to get fake adopters to come in and rescue all the pets they could. It nearly killed poor Bertie, losing her dear pet like that, and it ultimately did."

"I just heard about Bertie's death. I'm so sorry about your friend, Jenna."

"It was her heart."

"She had a heart attack?" Well, that was one less murder in Tahoe that needed to be solved.

"They'll call it that, but poor Bertie really died of a broken heart, thanks to that horrid Marx woman. I tried to work around her to rescue the dogs, but it was already too late for Gilda. When I found out what Rhoda had done, I confronted her and threatened to get her fired. We got into a shoving match, and when I pushed her back she fell and hit her head hard. When I realized she was dead, I panicked."

Panic was certainly an emotion I could appreciate at the moment.

Jenna wrung her hands as she talked, not really to me at all, but to herself, purging her guilty conscience as though that made everything she'd done all right. "I didn't know what to do, so I tried to cover up her death by making it look like TAILS did it. They already have such a bad reputation in the community, I figured the police would automatically pin the crime on them."

Who wouldn't suspect TAILS of foul play? I did, too. Tori made such a convenient target with her purple hair and posturing.

"So I dragged Rhoda's body into the chamber and turned on the gas. I confess it gave me immense pleasure to do the same thing to her as she'd done to poor Gilda and all those other helpless pets." Jenna placed her hand over the switch as she spoke, which made me increasingly nervous.

"If her death was accidental, Jenna, then the courts will show leniency, but if you kill me, you'll get murder one for sure. I know you're confused right now, but please stop and think about what you're doing."

"There's no way out of this for me. It's

too late. Too late."

"You do have a way out of this. Listen to me, Jenna. You do!"

Clearly I didn't, however. I watched in horror as Jenna prepared to depress the switch to start the flow of deadly gas into the chamber. "Jenna, stop! You know you wouldn't do it to a dog. Please don't do it to me. Let me out of here!"

I heard a hissing sound. Jenna had turned on the gas! I couldn't smell anything, but you can't smell carbon monoxide. It's odorless.

"Help! Help me!" I pounded on the panel and screamed as loud as I could, but I realized that I was inside a device that was designed to muffle the desperate cries of the dying. Who would ever be able to hear me inside this doggone chamber of death?

CHAPTER 48

Cruiser was baying his dear old heart out from within the holding cell, where dogs were contained briefly before it was their turn to take the Big Sleep. What must it be like to watch your brethren being dragged to their deaths but be powerless to save them or yourself? Like them, Cruiser couldn't get free from his prison. He had come to my rescue so many times before, but it looked like it was my turn to find out whether or not euthanasia really was a "good death," as the Greeks say.

I heard the steady hiss of gas leaking into the chamber. Soon my lungs would be robbed of life-giving oxygen and within seconds I would be dead. I imagined I heard the sound of a basset duo howling in chorus. Was it the sound of Cruiser's distressed cries I heard echoing through the halls of the shelter? Or was I back at the Basset Waddle again judging the Best Howl contest? I feared that, like Gilda, I might be headed for the last Waddle across the Bridge.

As I pounded on the chamber walls in the hope of being freed, I was vaguely aware of the percussive sound of a door banging open. Then I heard a familiar bark, but it wasn't Cruiser's. Even through my terror, I recognized the sound as that of a certain crazy dog named Calamity.

Jenna turned to see what all the commotion was about, but her reaction was too slow for Calamity, who was younger and speedier than her pack mate, Cruiser. Faster than a basset can flick a dollop of drool on a divan, she reared up on my assailant, boxing at her like a kangaroo with her paws, knocking Jenna right off her feet. I heard a loud thud as her head connected hard with the concrete. Jenna lay stretched on the floor like an old hound dog on the hearth, out cold and not stirring a muscle.

Calamity reared up on the chamber and scratched at the viewing panel to get to me. Now I understood how the paw prints Skip and his team had lifted from this contraption had gotten there. I guessed that Rhoda's pal, Spirit, had known she was trapped in here and had done the same thing Calamity was doing now. Perhaps that was why he had looked so downcast the day I first saw him at the shelter lying beside Rhoda's desk. Heck, even Adolf Hitler's German shepherd dog, Blondie, was devoted to her fuehrer. Only a dog could love someone like him or Rhoda Marx. The next face I saw peering at me through the panel of the chamber was a welcomed one that I loved more than anyone else's on earth besides Cruiser's, of course. It was Nona's sweet countenance, which appeared to me as an angel of mercy.

"Mom! Hold on. I'm getting you out of there right now."

Nona turned off the flow of gas, flipped the latches, and opened the chamber door, freeing me. She helped me to my feet, which I could barely feel after being cramped up inside there. My legs wobbled like two elastic bands beneath me. Nona went over to Cruiser's cell and opened the door to free him, too.

"I've never been so glad to see anyone in my life. Thank heavens you arrived when you did."

"I got worried when you didn't come back right away with Cruiser. I knew something must be wrong. Are you all right?"

"I will be."

"Looks like we arrived just in time."

"I'll say! What a good girl you are, Calamity!"

Now that was something Calamity hadn't heard too often in her life, but this time she had rightly earned her accolades and was deserving of the title of Good Dog. She waddled over to me for a pet and gave me a thorough sniffing as I stroked her silky brown coat. At first I thought she was checking me over to make sure I was all right, and that may have been the case. But I realized I might have also borne the pungent scent of fear and death from all the animals that had met their fate in that chamber, as I too nearly had.

Calamity's hindquarters were aquiver, but her puzzling reaction had nothing to do with the scent of my clothing. Something else was causing this strange behavior, and it was evidently something only a dog could detect with its keen senses, for when I glanced over at Cruiser I saw that he was also exhibiting the same strange reaction as Calamity's to something unseen in our midst.

Nona had alerted Skip on her cell phone on her way over to the shelter. This was one time I could forgive her for breaking the law about dialing and driving. The sheriff and his ravishing Rusty were quick to arrive on the scene. I was glad to learn she had decided not to pursue her harassment case against the department, and they didn't take any punitive action against her. Either Skip was more persuasive than I gave him credit for, or she had proved to them she could do her job and keep her privates private. Whatever their reasons, the sheriff's department let sleeping dogs lie and kept her on the force. She and Skip were a team again, not to mention an item, and they weren't about to let this sleeping dog lie. It was time to round up the pup perp and officially close this doggone case. Rusty smacked the cheeks of the unconscious woman to bring her around.

Jenna moaned in pain and began to stir. Now fully conscious, she sat up and rubbed the back of her head where a goose egg formed. Rusty did the cuffing while Skip read Jenna her rights before taking her into custody. Jenna had sealed her fate when she turned on the gas while I was inside the gas chamber. The only reason I was still alive to see justice done was because the CO tank was empty. The fact that she had not made sure to check the tank first carried no weight in the eyes of the law, however. Her sentence might have been lighter for Rhoda's accidental death, but her attempted murder of yours truly carried a stiffer penalty for which she would be punished to the full extent of the law. What sympathy I might have felt for her motives on behalf of homeless pets had dissipated when she entrapped Cruiser and then me inside a chamber of death.

Chapter 49

I was the last living thing ever to see the inside of the euthanasia chamber because its use was forthwith banned at the newly renovated no-kill Lakeside Animal Shelter Cruiser and I were touring today with its new manager, Amanda Peabody.

Two kittens batted playfully at each other inside a new state-of-the art cat colony with clear Plexiglas cages. Others climbed on a kitty condo. A husky and a lab cavorted with each other while an old coonhound lounged on a comfy sofa inside a large windowed play area strewn with toys. Volunteers chatted with shelter visitors, answering their questions and holding relaxed meet-and-greets in ambient private rooms where potential adopters could interact with the animals in peaceful surroundings. Hold times for all pets, licensed or not, had been increased from three days to three weeks, giving owners plenty of time to reclaim their pet before putting it up for adoption or fostering with Found Hounds or other rescue groups until placed in a loving home. What had happened to Gilda would never happen again. In fact, they had renamed the adoption branch of the shelter Gilda's Adoption Center.

"They've done wonders with this place, Amanda. It looks nothing like the old shelter."

"Lakeside Shelter has been transformed inside and out."

"So I can see."

"How did you get the money for all these wonderful improvements? I thought that they would be a long time coming with the current budget constraints."

"Thanks to fundraisers and a generous bequest from the Abigail Haversham Tahoe Trust she provided for in her estate, we were able to buy up some adjacent property to expand the size of the shelter. We've increased the quantity and dimensions of kennels and added a state-of-the art spay/neuter clinic, but as you can see, we have also improved on what was already here. The cages are now visitor friendly. Pets can be easily viewed by prospective adopters through one-way glass without even having to enter the kennel area, so it's not so stressful for the animals."

Lakeside now looked less like a lockdown and more like an alpine pet resort worthy of Lake Tahoe. I was pleased to see that everything possible had been done to make the animals' hopefully brief stay there more pleasant.

"We have hired new staff who are well qualified and better suited to their jobs, unlike some who worked here before."

"Yes, I know." Amanda didn't have to say their names aloud. I was just as glad as she was that they were no longer here.

"With plenty of staff on hand to do adoptions, deal with people bringing in animals, and other customer services duties, we're better able to focus on feeding and caring for the animals and maintaining the shelter. All the kennels are sanitized every day, and we make sure that all water and chemicals are cleaned up and safely stored before customers arrive."

"I noticed the difference the moment I entered the shelter."

"Smells a lot better now, huh? I'm sure Cruiser agrees, don't you, boy?"

"Roo, roo!" The only doggy scent his sensitive nose detected now was that of the treats stashed in a jar on the counter. Amanda offered Cruiser a biscuit, which he accepted

without a moment's hesitation.

Noticeably absent from the new shelter was Calamity's old nemesis, Rex. He'd not only been fired from his job, but was jailed and heavily fined after it was discovered he'd been selling animals from the shelter to pet shops and research labs, though he denied ever having unleashed any strays on the community. The judge decreed that he account for every cent of the money he had made from the sale of the animals and donate it to Tahoe's new animal shelter.

At least I knew it wasn't TAILS activists who were responsible for the shelter break-ins. They had thankfully redirected their attention to protesting at research labs to liberate the animals there. Though I still wasn't too fond of Tori or her troublemakers, I hoped they would eventually succeed in their goal of ending animal experimentation once and for all.

The shelter had hired new animal care officers, whose attention to animal welfare in the community could continue. Updated transport vehicles made the ride to the shelter more comfortable and less stressful for strays. The objective now wasn't to catch 'em and kill 'em, as Rhoda's had been, but to rescue animals from deplorable living conditions, cite and prosecute cruel or neglectful owners, attend to sick and injured animals, and protect them from further injury and distress. Humane officers were specially trained to assess a stray animal's condition in the field and provide preliminary medical assistance to sick or injured dogs and cats until the animal could be transported to a veterinarian for treatment. A team of humane educators now made regular rounds in Tahoe, including at schools where children were taught early lessons in kindness to animals and the responsible care of pets.

"We have a large exercise yard and several homey get-acquainted rooms," Amanda added. "We also have raised beds for the dogs, better security, and surveillance cameras installed inside and out. We've hired more vets and animal behaviorists to rehabilitate the pets we take in so they're more adoptable. We even pipe in music to help calm the animals."

"A little mutt music, eh?"

She laughed. "It's recorded especially for dogs, but the cats seem to enjoy it, too."

"I have to admit the place is a lot more peaceful than it was when Calamity was kenneled here. I'll have to try some of that music at home."

"How is your latest foster doing, by the

way? Have you found an adopter for her yet?"

"Why, yes. I believe I have."

"That's great! Who took her?"

"My daughter did. Nona fell in love with Calamity from the get-go, and the feeling was mutual. They bonded almost instantly. Calamity has a new home with her in San Francisco."

"How is Nona doing, anyway? I heard she had a health scare."

"She did, but she's fine now. Fortunately, the tumor was benign and has completely disappeared without her having to undergo any surgery."

"That's wonderful, Beanie! They have so many new ways in medicine."

"True, but sometimes it's the old ways that work best."

Nona probably wasn't as likely as I was to claim that Native American medicine had any part in her healing, but I was glad my daughter was learning a new respect for traditional Indian ways. If more of our youngsters in the tribe can do the same, things may finally improve for the Washoe in Tahoe. Of course, I couldn't discount the healing power of a pet. Calamity deserved some credit, too. There's just no better medicine than the love of a devoted dog.

"I'm glad she's going to be okay, Elsie."

"Yep, Nona has a new lease on life and also on a larger apartment near Golden Gate Park, so Calamity will get lots of exercise. Maybe she won't be so crazy now that she's settled in a permanent home with Nona."

"That will be good for her, I'm sure. How is Cruiser handling his pack mate's absence?"

"He's fine with it. He likes being king of his own castle, you know. He tolerates other dogs in his territory for a little while, but he really prefers being an only dog. He likes being the center of attention. Of course, Nona will bring Calamity along with her whenever she visits, so he isn't completely rid of her."

Nor was I. I didn't say it out loud, but I knew what we were both thinking. Amanda had met Calamity too, so she knew what she was like. An occasional Calamity at the house was better than having that crazy hound around all the time. Cruiser's Yum-Yum Nook was all his for the raiding again, at least for the time being.

CHAPTER 50

Dog-shaped clouds chased a yellow ball sun along the western horizon as Lakeside Shelter's grand opening celebration was winding down. Most of the other visitors had already left, and many went home with a new canine or feline friend.

There had been many adoptions on the opening day of Lake Tahoe's new shelter. Seeing the animals looking happier and healthier in their shelter surroundings made them more appealing to prospective adopters. Everyone who remembered what our community's animal shelter had once been like under Rhoda Marx felt confident that there would be many more happy endings for the homeless pets that came to stay here in comfort and safety for a little while before finding their forever homes with people who would give them the full measure of love that should be every pet's birthright. Calamity was one of the lucky ones that had been re-homed, thanks to the efforts of Amanda Peabody and others who went to great lengths to ensure their survival against all odds.

As Cruiser and I made our way down a quiet corridor of the new shelter, we had no choice but to walk past the same kennel that had once briefly held the ill-fated basset hound named Gilda. The cage was now assigned a different number and was presently unoccupied, or so I thought until we approached it. Cruiser froze in his tracks, his attention trained on something inside the haunted kennel. Had someone left some stray crumbs of kibble or a biscuit behind? No, that wasn't it. I couldn't see anything that would elicit such a reaction in him.

"Come on, boy. It's time for us to go home now."

No matter how much I coaxed him to follow me, Cruiser wouldn't budge an inch from the spot. His tail began to helicopter in a friendly greeting. He let out a friendly bark and kept barking insistently at something inside the vacant kennel.

Roo, roo! I was puzzled by his odd reaction. What did he see in there that I couldn't? His focus was now trained on the hallway. I tried tugging on his leash to lead him away from the spot, but he resisted, standing his ground doggedly, as only a basset can. Something was definitely there, all right.

"What is it, Cruiser?"

Through a window, the late afternoon sun illuminated the corridor. Then I saw it, too! Cruiser lifted his nose and bayed at the vaporous apparition that waddled slowly away from us. With white-tipped tail carried gaily aloft in true hound fashion, the phantom of Lakeside Animal Shelter dissolved in golden beams of light. Gilda had gone home at last.

ABOUT THE AUTHOR

Sue Owens Wright is an award-winning writer of both fiction and nonfiction about dogs. She is a fancier and rescuer of basset hounds, which are frequently featured in her books and essays. She is a nine-time nominee for the Maxwell, awarded annually by the Dog Writers Association of America to the best writer on the subject of dogs. She has twice won the Maxwell Award and also earned special recognition from the Humane Society of the United States for her writing on animal welfare issues. She lives in Northern California with her husband and bassets.

The employees of Thorndike Press hope you have enjoyed this Large Print book. All our Thorndike, Wheeler, and Kennebec Large Print titles are designed for easy reading, and all our books are made to last. Other Thorndike Press Large Print books are available at your library, through selected bookstores, or directly from us.

For information about titles, please call:
(800) 223-1244

or visit our Web site at:
http://gale.cengage.com/thorndike

To share your comments, please write:
Publisher
Thorndike Press
10 Water St., Suite 310
Waterville, ME 04901